JOURNEY TO AMERICA

Aniela Kaminski's Story

A Voyage from Poland During World War II

JOURNEY TO AMERICA

Aniela Kaminski's Story

A Voyage from Poland During World War II

CLARE PASTORE

BERKLEY JAM BOOKS, NEW YORK

JOURNEY TO AMERICA: ANIELA KAMINSKI'S STORY:
A VOYAGE FROM POLAND DURING WORLD WAR II

A Berkley Jam Book / published by arrangement with the author

PRINTING HISTORY
Berkley Jam hardcover edition / March 2001
Berkley Jam paperback edition / November 2002

Cover illustration by Heidi Oberheide.
Cover design by Elaine Groh.

For information address: The Berkley Publishing Group, a division of Penguin Putnam Inc.,
375 Hudson Street, New York, New York 10014.

Visit our website at www.penguinputnam.com

ISBN: 0-425-18816-7

BERKLEY JAM BOOKS®
Berkley Jam Books are published by The Berkley Publishing Group,
a division of Penguin Putnam Inc.,
375 Hudson Street, New York, New York 10014.
BERKLEY JAM and its logo
are trademarks belonging to Penguin Putnam Inc.

PRINTED IN THE UNITED STATES OF AMERICA

10 9 8 7 6 5 4 3 2 1

This book is dedicated with love to my four kids:
Michael, Katherine, James and Nicholas

Author's Note

WHEN you read about foreign lands, it's fun to learn about different names. Sometimes, they are pronounced very differently than they are spelled. In this book, Aniela's name is pronounced "Ahn-YELL-ah" and Jadzia's name is pronounced "YAH-ja."

Chapter One

THE bell above the door jingled as Aniela Kaminski handed pork chops wrapped in brown paper to Mrs. Nowalski, a regular customer at her father's butcher shop. Aniela looked up and smiled when she saw her two best friends, Jadzia Kolbe and Edith Lukowicz enter the shop. Jadzia politely held the door open for Mrs. Nowalski to exit before she turned to Aniela.

"Do you want to see a movie today?" Jadzia asked. "It's called *San Francisco*."

"It's from America," Edith said excitedly. "With Clark Gable!"

Aniela loved American movies and thought Clark Gable was just wonderful. The cinema hardly ever showed movies from the United States. But she had other things to do today. She shook her head regretfully.

"I can't," she said. "First I have to help Papa here, then I have a piano lesson with Stefan."

Jadzia and Edith looked at each other and started to giggle.

"Oh, Stefan!" Edith sighed. "Your piano teacher is so handsome!"

"And so nice!" Jadzia added. "Who needs American movie stars when you have him for a teacher?"

Stefan Olczak lived in the apartment behind the butcher shop. He was a student at the University of Warsaw and in exchange for his room and board, he taught Aniela how to play the piano.

Aniela was about to agree he was wonderful when her father came out of the back room and handed her a tray of lamb chops.

"Wrap these nicely for Mrs. Kozal," Max Kaminski said. "And remember that she likes the string tied very loosely. It is difficult for her to open these packages with her rheumatism."

"Yes, Papa," Aniela replied. "I'll do a good job."

Papa smiled at her. He was a big man, but had a gentle voice and kind eyes. He looked so strong that, until he came out from behind the counter, no one would suspect that his leg was lame. Papa had taken a bullet in the knee during the Great War in 1918, and now he walked with a limp. He was all the family Aniela had in the world, since Mama had died when she was a little girl. Aniela loved him so much, and always wanted to make him happy.

"I know you'll do a good job," Papa said, and went back to the other room.

Aniela carefully wrapped the meat as she spoke with her friends. "What about Saturday for the movies?"

Edith shook her head. "That's the Sabbath, Aniela. I can't go to the movies that day."

"Oh, I'm sorry," Aniela said. "I forgot. And I can't go Sunday, of course. What about next week?"

"That would be great," Jadzia decided. "But not on Tuesday. There is going to be a meeting at the inn, and I have to mind the children."

Jadzia's parents owned a small hotel a few streets away. Her family lived on the top floors.

Edith nodded. "My parents are going to that meeting. They're going to discuss raising money to help the Polish Army."

This entire summer, the only thing the adults talked about was the threat of war. Germany had invaded Czechoslovakia, and the citizens of Poland were afraid that their homeland would be next. Everyone was nervous to think of Germany to the west, and Russia, with its big, powerful army, to the east.

Aniela finished tying the package, with the strings tied loosely just as Papa had said.

"Do you want to deliver this with me?" she asked her friends.

Both girls agreed, and they all set out to take the

package to Mrs. Kozal. She lived only a few blocks away, and the task was soon completed. As the girls walked back to the butcher shop, they chattered about the coming school year.

"My mother is going to let me buy a whole new outfit for the first day!" Jadzia exclaimed, her gray eyes sparkling. "Even a new pair of shoes!"

"Lucky you," Edith said. "I have to wear my sister's hand-me-down coat. It's green and I don't like green."

Suddenly, from around the corner, they heard shouts and a cry. They ran to see what was wrong. To their horror, they saw three teenagers attacking a young boy. They kicked him and pushed the little boy up against a building. One boy punched him hard on the arm, and the little boy cried out in pain.

"Get out of Poland, Jew!" the biggest boy shouted. "We don't want you here!"

"Oh, no!" Edith gasped. "That's my neighbor, Seth! He's only eight!"

The three hoodlums turned to face the girls. Aniela felt anger rise up inside of her. How could these young men attack a little boy? They were almost twice his size!

"Three against one!" she cried. "And all of you bigger! Shame on you!"

"What was that, Jew-lover?" the biggest boy asked. He had a sneer on his face as he walked toward Aniela and her friends.

Aniela stood her ground. Papa had always taught her to be brave.

"You heard what I said just fine," Aniela growled.

"Aniela, please don't," Edith said. Her voice shook. "You'll only make it worse!"

But Aniela bent to the ground and picked up a chunk of broken brick. She pulled her arm back, ready to throw the brick. Instead, a hand caught hold of her wrist. Aniela turned and was surprised to see Stefan. The leader of the thugs stared at the older man for a moment, as if trying to challenge him. Finally, though, he turned and gestured to his friends.

"Come on, let's go," the boy said.

"Yes, go," Stefan ordered, a fierce scowl on his face. "And don't let me see your faces in our neighborhood again!"

Edith hurried over to Seth, who looked as if he was trying hard not to cry. Stefan let go of Aniela's wrist. Aniela frowned at him. Her piano teacher held a pile of books in one arm. He had just come back from classes at the university.

"I had to try to stop them, Stefan," Aniela insisted.

"I know," Stefan said. His large brown eyes were sad. He shoved his glasses up the bridge of his nose, then pushed back a dark brown curl that had fallen over his forehead. "But there are so many like them in Warsaw now. And if you had thrown that brick, perhaps they would have hurt you. We live in a dangerous world, Aniela."

"Why do people have to be so cruel?" Jadzia asked. "Why do some hate the Jews so much? Edith and her family . . . well, they're such nice people!"

"Adolf Hitler teaches hatred, even to some of our fellow Poles," Stefan said. "We can only pray he doesn't gain more power."

Edith walked with Seth back toward them. She held Seth's hand, and the little boy stood very close to her.

"I'm going to walk Seth home," Edith said.

"I'll go with you," Jadzia offered.

"Please be careful, girls," Stefan said.

Both girls smiled shyly at the handsome young man. Jadzia tucked a strand of blonde hair into her kerchief, as if she wanted to make herself prettier.

"We will, Stefan," she promised.

Aniela said good-bye to her friends and walked back to the butcher shop with Stefan. She didn't really want to take her piano lesson now. How could she concentrate on the piano after seeing the terrible thing those boys did?

"Don't look so glum," Stefan advised. "If you let those boys make you sad, it's like letting them win. You should refuse to let their hatred poison your joy."

"But enjoying myself seems so wrong right now," Aniela protested. "Music seems so wrong!"

Stefan put an arm around her shoulders. "No, Aniela, music is right and good. And if you work even harder at your lessons, you'll show people like those boys you aren't afraid of them!"

Stefan's smile was so warm and encouraging that Aniela had to smile, too. Stefan was right. She wouldn't let those awful boys ruin her favorite thing to do. Instead, she went straight to the piano and sat down at the bench as soon as they arrived at Stefan's apartment. Stefan had a copy of Chopin's "Minute Waltz" open on the music stand. He gave Aniela a nod and she began to play. She did not even have to look at the notes. This was one of her favorite pieces and she knew it by heart. As her fingers flew over the keys, she gazed at a picture of her mother that sat on the piano in a silver frame. It showed Helena Kaminski in a beautiful white satin gown, seated at a grand piano. Aniela had asked if she could put a picture of her mother on the piano for inspiration during the lessons, and Stefan had agreed that it was a good idea.

"Mama was so beautiful," she said when she finished playing the last note. "I wish she were still alive."

"She was a fine pianist," Stefan said. "I had the pleasure of hearing her at the National Theater when I was younger. I think she would have been a great musician, perhaps even another Paderewski."

"Oh, what an honor to play there!" Aniela exclaimed. "It has the biggest stage in all of Europe."

"That's true," Stefan agreed, and picked up the photograph.

"You look like her," he remarked. "You have the same long curls in your brown hair, and the same dark, almond-shaped eyes."

Aniela smiled up at him. She thought her mother was very beautiful, so it was a great compliment to hear that she resembled her.

"Now, let's see if perhaps, one day, you'll play in

concert like she did," Stefan said. "Here's a new piece for you."

This was a work by Beethoven called "Minuet in G." Stefan helped her learn the notes, and she practiced the piece over and over until she felt comfortable with it. Aniela knew she did have a certain talent for the piano, which helped her to learn music quickly.

"Good work, Aniela," Stefan praised, and then he looked at the clock. "The lesson is over for today."

"Can't we do a little more?" Aniela asked hopefully. "I want to practice that last stanza again."

Stefan shook his head. "I have a big test in biology tomorrow," he explained, "I need time to study."

A little disappointed, Aniela thanked him for the lesson and said good-bye. She walked into the butcher shop just as Papa was locking up for the evening. He reached to pull down the shade, but his hand stopped midway. He gazed at something across the street.

"What is it, Papa?" Aniela asked. She came to stand at his side.

Papa pointed. "Something is wrong at Mr. Guzowski's bookshop."

Aniela looked into the shop through its large display window. Two men stood with Mr. Guzowski. One shook his fist and the other seemed to be shouting something. Then the first man grabbed the bookseller by the collar of his suit jacket and pulled him out of sight. The second man glanced out the window as if checking for possible witnesses. Before his eyes could catch sight of Aniela and her father, Papa quickly pulled down the window shade.

"What are they doing, Papa?" Aniela felt her stomach tighten with anxiety. She thought of those boys who had hurt Seth today, just because he was Jewish. Mr. Guzowski was Jewish, too. Was this more of the same?

"I don't know," Papa said, "but I mean to find out. Aniela, you go upstairs now."

"Papa, I want to come with you!"

Papa, who was always so soft-spoken, gave her a very stern look.

"Do as you're told, Aniela," he ordered.

She could not question Papa when he sounded like that. Aniela was scared, but still she climbed the stairs to their apartment, and went to her small but cozy bedroom. A quilt her grandmother had made many years ago covered the bed. There was a little white desk for her schoolwork and books, and an oak bureau for her clothes. Stuffed animals and dolls filled three shelves on the wall. Her American cousins had sent her a poster of the New York World's Fair, which gave the room a cheerful touch. Best of all, Aniela liked the big arched window, with its padded seat. She could see a lot through it, from the pointed rooftop of St. Hedwig's Church on the nearby corner, to the distant hills beyond the city. It was a beautiful view. But she did not care about the view today. She only cared about Papa and what would happen at the bookshop.

She knelt on the window seat and opened the window. She watched Papa limp quickly across the street and enter the bookshop. Aniela heard him call Mr. Guzowski's name, then a shout and a loud crash. And then Aniela saw Papa push one of the men from the store. Papa had the man's arm twisted behind his back. He gave the man a great shove.

"Stay away from here!" Papa cried. "Or next time that arm will snap in two!"

Aniela caught her breath. She had never seen Papa so angry.

The second man came up behind Papa. Aniela watched in horror as he lifted a heavy bookend over Papa's head. She opened her mouth to cry out to him, to warn him, but Papa must have heard the man because he ducked out of the way just in time. The man stumbled over him and dropped the bookend.

"Get out! Get out of Warsaw, and out of Poland! We don't need your hatred here!" Papa yelled.

"Fool!" the man cried. "You'll see what happens to Jew-lovers soon enough! You'll see!"

Papa moved as if to strike. The man backed away from him, then ran away shouting curses. His friend followed close behind. Papa looked up at Aniela's window. She felt a little embarrassed to realize he knew she'd be watching. But he wasn't angry. He gave her a little smile and a wave, to tell her all was well. Then he went into the bookshop again.

A few minutes later, Papa entered the apartment with Mr. Guzowski. The man held a handkerchief to his bleeding nose. His suit was torn and he had a black eye. Aniela was so furious she wanted to cry. Mr. Guzowski was an old man who had never hurt anyone!

"Do you want me to ring for the doctor?" Papa asked.

Mr. Guzowski shook his head. "I will be all right, Max."

"Aniela, run downstairs and get a raw steak for our friend," Papa said.

Aniela obeyed promptly. Papa helped the old man put the steak against his swollen eye. Aniela put on a pot of tea and began to prepare dinner. She listened as the adults spoke.

"Why do they do this?" Mr. Guzowski asked. "I am a Polish citizen. I don't want to fight with anyone!"

"Those men are but a few that are full of hate," Papa said.

"They hate me because I'm a Jew," Mr. Guzowski cried. "Just for that reason. What did I ever do to them? I don't even know them!"

"I think, perhaps," Papa replied, "that hatred works best between strangers."

Aniela thought Papa was very wise. If those men really knew the sweet old bookseller, would they have hurt him?

She brought a cup of tea to her neighbor. He smiled at her gratefully as he accepted it. The men talked about other things, from prices in the market to the threat of war. Finally, Mr. Guzowski bid them good-bye and went home. Aniela and Papa sat down to a dinner of kielbasa and potatoes.

"Papa, are we going to war?" Aniela asked as soon as Papa finished saying grace.

"Don't worry about that, little one," Papa said. "You are but a child and should leave those thoughts to adults. Just know that I will take care of you."

But Aniela did worry. Over the next days, it seemed to be all anyone would talk about. Customers came into the butcher shop to use the telephone to call relatives and make certain they were all right. People watched the skies as if waiting for enemy planes to appear out of the clouds. Papa bought two gas masks and showed Aniela how to use hers. He asked her to help him pack up their few valuables. They carefully wrapped Mama's crystal and fine china and put it into boxes full of straw. Papa carried them down into the cellar below the butcher shop. He did not say why he did this, but Aniela knew. If the Germans were to drop bombs as they had in Czechoslovakia, they would need to protect their precious heirlooms.

There was a lot of whispering in the weeks following, but the adults would say little to the children. And daily life resumed its regular pattern. Aniela took her piano lessons three times a week and prepared for the new school year. She went to the movies with her friends and had picnics in Lazienki Park. Sometimes, the three girls sat on the curb and watched as men in Polish Army uniforms walked by.

"They look so handsome," Jadzia commented. "My father and my brother have both enlisted. We're so proud of them!"

"My papa and two brothers joined, too," Edith said. "Mama cried and cried about it. But all the men want to fight these Nazis."

"I hope they don't have to fight at all," Aniela said quietly. "I don't want anyone to die."

The three girls fell silent. Maybe the soldiers were handsome in their uniforms, and maybe fighting for Poland was a glorious thing, but none of them wanted to imagine that a beloved father or brother might never come home again.

ONE bright August afternoon, Aniela came home from Jadzia's house and entered the butcher shop to see Papa counting money. It was more than she had ever seen him make in one day.

"You must have sold a lot today, Papa," she said. "I'm sorry I wasn't here to help you with such a crowd!"

Papa smiled at her. "This isn't from my customers. I took it out of the bank today."

"Why? Are we going to buy something new?"

"No, Aniela," Papa said. "Something tells me we'll need this one day soon. I just . . . well, I just feel better having my money here with me."

Aniela didn't understand why, since Papa had always said how strong and safe the bank was. But she did not question him.

JUST before dawn one morning, when Aniela was tucked deep under her quilt, she had a dream. She dreamed she was on a concert stage, wearing a white satin dress and playing Chopin on a grand piano. When she finished, the audience broke into thunderous applause. Aniela stood up to take a bow. Papa, looking handsome in a black tuxedo, clapped hardest of everyone. Next to him, Stefan began to call out her name. The audience joined in, and Aniela blushed with pride.

But then the shouting turned to screams! A man ran down the center aisle, waving his arms.

"They're bombing us! They're bombing us!"

Aniela jerked awake. Through her window, she could see a cloud of black smoke rising behind the pointed roof of the church. Instead of the shouts she'd heard in her dream, she now heard the horrible, high-pitched screams of an air raid siren. Suddenly, her door burst open.

"We're under attack, Aniela!" Papa cried. "There is no time to dress—just put on your robe and slippers! We must get to the air raid shelter!"

Quickly, Aniela obeyed her father. They met Stefan on the way downstairs.

Aniela's robe was hardly enough to keep her warm on this chilly September morning, but she was too afraid to notice the cold. Papa held her hand tightly as they rushed to the shelter, the basement of the town hall. Aniela screamed as planes soared over their heads, flying in V formation like demonic geese. A few moments later, they heard a crash as a bomb was dropped at the edge of the city.

As people hurried to the shelter, Polish troops raced into action in the hopes of saving Warsaw. Papa moved very fast in spite of his limp. By the time they got downstairs and huddled on the floor, he was panting with exhaustion. Aniela snuggled close to him, drawing her arms tight around him. Stefan peered closely at Papa, concern clear in his gaze.

"Are you all right, Mr. Kaminski?" he asked.

Papa nodded. "I'll be fine. Let me catch my breath."

Everyone stared up at the ceiling, as if they could see through it to the sky above.

"How could they do this to us?" Papa asked. "There was never even a declaration of war!"

"Do you think the Nazis care to fight by any rules?" Stefan asked, and no one could answer that.

"Papa, will they destroy everything?" Aniela asked.

Papa shook his head and sighed. "I don't know, Aniela."

Father Henryk, the priest from St. Hedwig's Church, spoke now.

"Perhaps it would be best to pray," he suggested.

"Yes, prayer is what we need now," said Rabbi Zorawska and he nodded to the Catholic priest. Father Henryk led his congregation in prayer, and then Rabbi Zorawska prayed with his own people. It was all they could do.

Hours passed. At last, the all clear sounded. Stefan put an arm around Aniela's shoulder as they followed

Papa and the others up the stairs to the street. Clouds of smoke filled the sky, but to everyone's relief, the main street had not been harmed. Everyone hurried to their shops and homes.

Aniela went up to her bedroom to get dressed. She looked out her window and saw that several buildings just a short distance away had been flattened to rubble. Swirls of smoke crawled up to the sky. Aniela gazed at the clouds in terror, afraid to see more planes. For now, though, all was silent.

After she dressed, she went to the calender on her wall and circled the date: September 1, 1939. It was the day, she knew, that her life had changed forever.

Chapter Two

ANIELA learned a new word that September: *blitz-krieg*. It was a German word meaning "lightning war." The Nazi attack on Poland was as swift, hard, and devastating as a bolt of lightning. The Polish troops simply did not have enough time to react. The German army seized Gdynia Harbor on the Baltic Sea, and continued to march south.

The people of Warsaw did what they could to prepare for Nazi attack. Bombs were dropped on the city almost every day, but the Polish army fought back bravely and kept Warsaw out of enemy hands. All the while, Papa tried his best to make a normal life for Aniela. She still went to school, played with her friends, and took her piano lessons. On several occasions, Stefan had to cut a lesson short when the air raid sirens warned of approaching enemy planes.

"You just wait until the rains come," Papa said. "There is no way the German tanks can move through thick Polish mud! Then our cavalry, our trained horsemen, will triumph!"

But the rains did not come, and the Germans easily moved over the hard ground. In Warsaw, children played in gas masks and shopkeepers piled sandbags. People stood in long lines at stores, including Papa's butcher shop, to buy what little food was available. It was hard to transport anything now that the roads were clogged with Polish men on their way to join their troops. Food and medical supplies were scarce. People were sick and hungry, and yet Aniela's neighbors refused to give up hope.

"We will fight, and we will drive these Nazis out of our homeland!" Papa insisted. "They will not take Warsaw!"

Citizens and military personnel alike fought to protect the city. But how long, Aniela wondered, could they keep Warsaw out of Nazi hands?

One day, as Aniela gazed out at the sky in search of planes, Stefan pulled down the window shade.

"Let the world out there go by for a while, Aniela," he said. "In here, only the music is important."

Aniela began to play Dvořák's "Largo." It was a sad song. She felt as if her own sadness poured out through her fingers and into the keys. She closed her eyes as she played. In her mind, there were pictures of children running through a field, as enemy planes zoomed overhead.

Aniela opened her eyes when she finished and turned to Stefan. He always had a comment for her. Sometimes, he told her ways to improve her work. Sometimes, he simply nodded and said it was "fine." But today, there were tears in his eyes, surprising Aniela. She had never seen a man cry before.

"Stefan, what's wrong?" she asked.

He blinked a few times before answering.

"Nothing, nothing at all," he said, his voice hoarse. "That was beautiful, Aniela. I don't think I've ever heard you play as well."

"As well as Mama did, maybe?" Aniela asked hopefully.

Now Stefan smiled. "As well as your mother, yes. Aniela, never give up your music. One day, I know you will be a fine pianist."

"I want to do that more than anything in the world," Aniela told him. "I want to wear a beautiful gown like the one in Mama's photograph, and play a white grand piano in a big concert hall."

"I'm sure you will," Stefan said. "Now, perhaps we can play something a little lighter? Let's see . . ."

He shuffled through the sheet music and set a copy of Chopin's "Military Polonaise" on the piano. Aniela played as Stefan tapped a pencil on the edge of the piano, in time to the music. This was a marching tune, and now she imagined Polish soldiers marching in a grand victory parade.

"The soldiers will make the Nazis go away, won't they?" she asked when she finished.

"I'm certain that we'll do our best," Stefan said. "I know that I will."

"And then we can . . ."

Aniela stopped. She realized what Stefan had just said.

"What do you mean, you will?" she asked.

"Aniela, all strong and able men have been asked to join the Polish Army," Stefan said. "I signed up a few days ago."

Aniela swirled around on the piano bench until she faced her teacher.

"You can't go, Stefan!" she cried. "I don't want you to go! Who will teach me? What if something happens to you?"

"I have to go, Aniela," he replied. "It is my duty as a Polish citizen to fight these monsters. But I don't plan to be gone long at all. The British and the French have declared war on Germany. It is only a matter of time before they send in troops to help us. We will drive Hitler and his armies away and live in peace again."

"When will that happen, Stefan?"

"I don't know," Stefan said. "Aniela, that's enough lessons for today. Why don't you go help your father?"

"There isn't much for him to do," Aniela said with a frown. "He hardly gets any meat to sell now."

She stood up and left Stefan's apartment. She went down to the butcher shop, but as she suspected, her father did not need her help and he urged her to go play.

As she passed the line of customers hoping to buy the little meat Papa had to sell, a woman took hold of her shoulder. It was Mrs. Sokop, who lived near Lazienki Park. She smiled at Aniela, but her eyes were sad. She reached a gnarled, arthritis-stricken hand to Aniela's face and stroked her cheek.

"Such beautiful music you play, dear Aniela," she said. "It brings me such joy to hear it!"

"Yes, it makes the time go by more quickly," said Mr. Sawicki, the man who lit the street lamps each evening.

Everyone in line agreed that Aniela's music was wonderful, and begged her to never give it up. Aniela looked at Papa, who gave her a little wink. She felt very proud as she left the shop. Stefan was right. Music was a good thing in these bad times, and she would never stop playing.

Her bicycle was locked on a pipe in front of the house. Aniela knelt down to open it. Next door, Mrs. Ryzop was taping the glass windows of her dress shop. Great big Xs partially blocked the view of the mannequins inside. This would help save the glass if bombs were dropped. Mrs. Ryzop waved when she saw Aniela. Aniela stood up with the chain and lock in her hand.

"Where are your friends today?" Mrs. Ryzop asked.

"Jadzia has gone to visit her aunt," Aniela said. "I'm going to Edith's house now."

Mrs. Ryzop glanced up at the sky.

"It isn't safe for children to be in the streets alone these days," she said.

Aniela knew she was worried about another bombing.

"I'll be all right, Mrs. Ryzop," she reassured her. "Edith's house is just three streets away."

"You'd better hurry, then," Mrs. Ryzop urged. "It's Friday night, and it's almost sundown. They'll be preparing for the Sabbath."

"Thank you, Mrs. Ryzop, I will," Aniela said, and she pedaled away.

Aniela loved to bicycle through the city. She always enjoyed its colorful buildings and pretty trees and flowers. But today, she only saw buildings that had fallen to the Nazi bombs and piles of rubble everywhere. A starving dog had made a home for itself under an overturned car. It growled at her as she passed. Aniela noticed the roof of one house had peeled back from an explosion, like a turned page in a book. She remembered that an elderly couple had died there. She saw abandoned homes with twisted shutters and shattered windows. There were so many reminders of the war that she was glad when she reached her friend's house.

Edith led her into the kitchen. Mrs. Lukowicz and her daughters rushed about as they prepared for the Sabbath. Edith was wearing a pretty white dress and she had pulled her hair back with a blue bow. She held a blue-and-white china platter of gefilte fish in her hands.

"It must be fun to have such a special meal each week," Aniela said.

"I like it," Edith told her as she set the platter on the table. "Mama is a wonderful cook."

Aniela grinned. "I know. I like her challah bread best of all."

Edith leaned closer to her and whispered, "Mama is sad today. She is so worried, with Papa and my brothers gone from our home. We hear so many horrible stories about how Hitler hates the Jews."

"He's an ogre," Aniela said with a fierce scowl. "Stefan says the British and French will help us drive him away. Do you know what, Edith?"

"What?"

"Stefan joined the army, too. He told me today."

Edith bowed her head and shook it slowly. "It makes me want to cry. I don't want anything to happen to my papa, or my brothers, or Stefan!"

"I'll say a million prayers for them this week," Aniela vowed.

"We'll say them at our meal tonight," Edith said.

Mrs. Lukowicz came in and placed a pair of beautiful silver candlesticks on the table. She usually had a friendly greeting for Aniela, but tonight she simply gave her a nod as she inserted a pair of white candles into the candlesticks.

"Edith, it's growing late," she said. "I don't think Aniela should ride home in the dark these days."

"I'm leaving now, Mrs. Lukowicz," Aniela said and stood up. "School starts on Monday, Edith. I'll see you then!"

"I hope we get Mrs. Kabatz this year," Edith said. "I don't want that nasty old Mr. Augustyn."

"I just want to be in the same class. Good-bye, Edith!" She gave her friend a quick hug.

Mrs. Lukowicz and Edith stood in the door and watched as she pedaled away. She turned to wave to them. Mrs. Lukowicz had never worried about any of the girls before the Germans invaded Poland. How Aniela hated the Germans! She hated the way things had changed, the way people had to live in fear now.

As she turned onto her street, the great blast of an air raid horn made her gasp. She almost lost control of her bicycle, but managed to keep steady even as her neighbors ran for the air raid shelter. Papa rushed out the door of the butcher shop, wiping his hands on his apron.

"Just leave the bicycle, Aniela!" he shouted over the sirens.

Aniela dropped her bicycle on the sidewalk in front of the butcher shop. Papa took her by the hand, and they followed a crowd to the nearby school. There was an air raid shelter in its basement. It was already so crowded with people, Aniela and Papa had to step over a few of their neighbors to find a spot.

Everyone crouched down in the dimly lit room. Papa kept an arm around Aniela's shoulder. Aniela bit her lip and wondered if this would be the day when the Nazi bombs finally destroyed Warsaw. But after a short time, the all clear sounded. People shuffled back up to the street and to their homes. It was almost dark, and Mr. Sawicki began to light the street lamps.

"Safe for now," Papa sighed. "Come, Aniela. It's time for dinner."

ANIELA worried that the Nazis would attack again, but for the next few days all was quiet. Her spirits perked up on the first day of school when she learned that Edith and Jadzia were both in her class. At lunchtime, they shared a spot under a big oak tree at the corner of the schoolyard.

"I'm so glad we have Mrs. Kabatz!" Jadzia exclaimed. "It's going to be a wonderful year."

"A year of air raid drills, I think," Aniela said. "Each time those planes come, I'm so afraid it's the end of us."

Edith shook her head. "I won't think like that. Mama says we must win this war! My father and brothers must come home soon!"

They had already had a raid that morning. All three girls looked up at the sky, but there was nothing to see now except fluffy white clouds.

"Radio Poland says the British and French are still trying to make peace," Aniela said. "But the announcer on the radio wonders when they will really help us. Why did they declare war, but they don't send troops our way?"

"Mama doesn't let me listen to the news," Jadzia

said. "She says I shouldn't have to worry about things like that."

"Papa also tells me not to worry," Aniela said as she peeled a hard-boiled egg. "But I can't help myself."

"Sometimes I wish I didn't even live in Poland," Edith said.

"Edith!" Jadzia said with a gasp. "I love our country, don't you?"

Edith bit into an apple. "Of course I do. But I don't love the people who do mean things to the Jews. I want to go someplace where everyone is nice."

"I don't think there is such a place," Aniela said.

"Maybe America," Jadzia decided. "They say that everyone is the same there. There are no rich people and no poor people. No one goes hungry. And there is no hate."

Aniela frowned. "I don't believe you."

"Then why do so many people go there?" Jadzia asked.

"I don't know." Aniela shrugged. "But I'll ask my Papa about America tonight. We have cousins there. Papa will know all about it."

AFTER dinner, as usual, Papa settled into his big chair with his pipe and his newspaper. Aniela did her homework at the kitchen table. In the background, Radio Poland offered news of the front lines, mixed in with the music of various artists. Whenever the announcer came on, Aniela tilted her head to listen. She hoped to hear of a grand victory by the Polish army. But it was all bad news.

Finally, when she was done with her homework, she packed her book bag and went into the living room.

"Papa, what is America like?" she asked.

Papa folded his newspaper and put it to the side. Aniela saw the big headline: KRAKOW UNDER SIEGE. She turned her head away from it. She sat down on the couch and tucked her feet up under her skirt.

"Ahhh . . . America." Papa sighed. "Such a beautiful place, little one! I took your mother there many years ago to visit her sister in Chicago. That would be your aunt Elzie. We arrived in New York City, first, and spent a few days there. I could not even begin to tell you of all the things we saw there! You had to strain your eyes to see the tops of some of the buildings."

"Did they look like mountains, Papa?" Aniela asked. "That's what I heard."

Papa laughed. "Yes, they did, indeed! Oh, but the most wonderful thing was the Statue of Liberty. She is so beautiful that people wept at the sight of her."

"I read about it in my history book," Aniela said.

"Your mother loved Carnegie Hall best," Papa continued. "I took her to a concert there. We had hoped that one day she might play on that stage."

He bowed his head and shook it a little, because the memory of her beautiful mother always made him sad. Then he looked at Aniela again and resumed speaking.

"We took a train from New York to Chicago. There

was another grand city! Your uncle Stanislaus and aunt Elzbieta live in a small town in its suburbs."

"It sounds very nice," Aniela said wistfully.

Papa took his pipe and tobacco pouch from its stand. As he filled it, he asked, "Would you like to go to America, someday?"

"Oh yes, Papa! I would like that very much. Jadzia tells me there are no hateful people there, but I'm sure that she exaggerates. But I would still love to see America."

Papa laughed a little bit. "Jadzia is a dreamer. But she is mostly right. There isn't as much hatred as there is here."

"Then I think Edith and her family should go, too," Aniela declared.

Papa sucked on his pipe and turned to stare out the window. It had started to rain outside, but even in the mist they could see the dark tendrils of smoke rising from nearby burned buildings. Aniela noticed her father had a grave expression in the reflection of the window.

"Yes, Edith and her family," he said. "I pray that all will go well for them."

He picked up his newspaper again.

"Now, Aniela, it's time for you to be off to bed."

"Good night, Papa," Aniela said, and bent to kiss his cheek.

"Good night, little one," Papa replied. He opened his newspaper and began to read.

As Aniela dressed for bed, she thought about

America. It truly did sound like a little bit of heaven on Earth. Wouldn't it be fun to visit Aunt Elzie, Uncle Stanislaus and her cousins one day?

But when she turned off the light, something else Papa said came to haunt her: *I pray that all will go well for them.* What could Papa have meant by that? Why did he sound so worried for Edith and her family?

Chapter Three

ANIELA sat in the seat nearest the door of Mrs. Kabatz's classroom. She chewed on a pencil and worked on a long division problem. Behind her, Jadzia sighed with frustration. Jadzia did not like math very much, while Aniela found it easy. She thought she would go to Jadzia's house this afternoon to help her with her homework. Maybe Edith could come, too. Mrs. Kolbe might have some babka to eat. Aniela was thinking how delicious it would taste, when the air raid siren blared out.

At once, the students stopped their work and stood up.

"Single file, children," Mrs. Kabatz ordered, "and no talking!"

Aniela was the first in line. Mrs. Kabatz moved in

front of her and waved the children on. They muttered among themselves despite their teacher's order for silence. Jadzia leaned closer to Aniela to speak.

"I hope the planes aren't over the school," she whispered.

Aniela prayed she was right. It had been almost four weeks since the Nazis first bombed Warsaw. So many other towns and cities had already fallen to them. They had kept Warsaw out of Nazi hands for twenty-seven days. Could they keep up the fight?

The bomb shelter was in the basement of the school, where the boilers rumbled and old books and papers were kept in storage. Aniela hated it down there. Cobwebs laced the corners, and as she huddled against the wall she was certain that a spider would come out and crawl into her hair.

Some of the boys started to joke with each other until a teacher hushed them.

"We'll be upstairs again in a few minutes," said a girl named Maryla.

But an hour went by, then two hours, and the younger children began to cry for their mothers. They could hear horrible noises up above: loud explosions, the engines of low-flying planes, and crashing sounds they could not identify.

"What can we do, Mrs. Kabatz?" Aniela asked.

Mrs. Kabatz held a little boy in her lap. He sucked on his thumb and stared at the furnace.

"All we can do now is pray for our city, and our people," Mrs. Kabatz said. There were tears in her eyes.

Aniela looked around and saw that some of the other teachers were also crying.

Many people had closed their eyes and were murmuring prayers. Aniela felt a tap on her shoulder. It was Edith, who had crawled across the room to be with her other two friends.

"I'm so scared," Edith said.

"Me, too," Jadzia agreed.

Aniela took both of their hands and the three held tightly to each other.

And then, at last, blessed silence. Aniela held her breath. Was it over? Could they finally go outside? But what would they find?

"I really don't think I want to go up there," she said. "I don't want to see it."

The principal, Mr. Pulaski, hushed them. He held up a hand and everyone listened. Minutes passed. The silence was total, and almost as frightening as the horrible noises above had been. Then the furnace clicked on, and a few children screamed.

"It's all right!" Mr. Pulaski cried out.

The all clear finally sounded. The teachers led the children back upstairs again. They were given orders to go directly home. But when the first group of children exited the old brick building, they could only stand in stunned silence. Jadzia burst into tears and hugged Edith.

"Sweet God," Aniela whispered. "What happened to our city?"

As far as they could see, only the school remained

standing. There was nothing left of the row of houses across the street but smoking rubble. The park next door had burned, and fires still crackled among its fallen trees. A mangled, blackened car rocked back and forth on its top like an overturned tortoise. Sunlight glistened on broken shards of glass.

"What about my mama?" Edith cried. "What about my sisters?"

She ran off, calling out as if her family could hear her. Aniela and Jadzia stared at each other for a shocked moment before they, too, ran to find their families. Aniela was terrified for her father. Her eyes were so blinded with tears of fright and worry that she did not see when Jadzia turned the corner to her own house.

The entrance to Aniela's street was blocked by the remains of blasted buildings. The shoe repair, a hotel, and two restaurants were gone now. Aniela climbed carefully over the debris. She stumbled and almost fell onto the broken red-and-white pole that had once sat in front of the barbershop, but managed to save herself at the last moment. When she climbed down the other side of the strange mountain, she saw that the opposite end of the street had been miraculously spared. Even her own home!

"Papa!" she screamed. *"Papa, where are you?"*

And then she saw him. He stepped out the door of the butcher shop and held out his big, wonderful arms. Aniela ran into them and hugged him tight. She could not stop sobbing for several minutes.

"Oh, Papa!" she wept. "What have they done? They have destroyed our beautiful city!"

"Warsaw has fallen at last," Papa said. He pushed her gently away and held her face in his big hands. "But we are alive, Aniela. Alive and well! We must thank God for that!"

Aniela did not feel much like thanking God for anything right then, but she kept silent. She looked past her father into the butcher shop. The shelves had been knocked over by shock waves and meat was scattered everywhere. She saw then that the door to Stefan's apartment was open.

"What about Stefan, Papa?" she asked. "Where is he?"

"He was not here when the klaxons rang," Papa said. "He had gone to one of his meetings."

At that moment, Mr. Guzowski and Mrs. Ryzop joined them.

"What to do now?" Mrs. Ryzop asked. "My dresses stink of smoke!"

"And my books are like garbage now," Mr. Guzowski said.

Papa heaved a big, deep sigh. "What is there to do? What is there to do but to rebuild again, to save what we can?"

And so, joined by others in the street, they began to clean up the debris. They moved in silent shock. Aniela picked up a broom and began to sweep. She could hear the sounds of ambulance and police sirens nearby.

Papa studied the meat that had fallen. He shook his head.

"Ruined," he said. "I can't sell this to my customers."

He threw it all into a trash bin. Aniela bit her lip so she would not cry again. How would Papa earn money with no meat to sell?

"If you clutch that broom any harder, Aniela," said a familiar voice behind her, "you'll snap it in two."

"Stefan!"

Aniela dropped the broom and turned to embrace him fiercely. "I was so worried!"

"I'm all right," he said. "I was with friends."

He looked around the butcher shop and shook his head sorrowfully. "I'm sorry about this, Mr. Kaminski."

Her father shrugged. "What can one do against such an enemy? We can only try to start again."

Stefan walked into his apartment. Aniela picked up the broom and continued to sweep. She heard a rumbling noise in the distance and prayed it wasn't another group of bombers.

Stefan came out again. "My things are all right. Just a few broken vases."

He held out the photograph of Aniela's mother. The frame was bent and the glass cracked.

"I thought you would want this," he said. "I think you should keep it close to you now."

"Thank you, Stefan," Aniela replied gratefully. "The piano is all right, isn't it?"

"Yes." Stefan nodded. "You'll be able to play again."

Aniela wasn't sure she would ever feel like playing. Then she looked at the photograph of her mother and knew that if Mama had been alive she would have wanted Aniela to continue with her music. But, for now, there was much work to do. Aniela carefully removed the broken glass, then set the photograph on the counter.

The rumbling noise grew louder, and the men went to the doorway to look down the street. Aniela set her broom against the counter and joined them. Her eyes widened to see something like a fat, green dinosaur rolling toward them. It was a panzer, squat and ugly and menacing. The tank was decorated with red-and-white flags emblazoned with black swastikas. They made Aniela think of broken crosses.

Another tank rolled onto the street, followed by several jeeps. Infantrymen came next, their faces hard and stern under round green helmets. Aniela looked up at Papa and saw his eyes had filled with tears. At that moment, she knew all hope was lost. Warsaw now belonged to the Germans.

The two tanks rolled over the mountain of debris at the end of the street and disappeared around a corner. The jeeps stopped in front of the toy store, one front wheel crushing a doll that had been thrown in the blast. A man in a fancy black uniform got out and began to shout things through a megaphone. Because he spoke German, Aniela did not understand him.

"What is he saying, Papa?" she asked.

But Papa did not speak German, either.

Stefan listened hard, then translated for them.

"He is telling us we are now under German rule," Stefan said. "We are prisoners of the Third Reich, and . . ."

"What's the Third Reich?" Aniela asked.

Papa shushed her. Now the German commander began to speak in Polish.

"People of Warsaw!" he shouted. "You are now prisoners of the Third Reich, under German rule! Regulations will be posted and rules strictly enforced! Any deviation will be punished severely! Dissidents will be shot!"

Aniela was surprised when Mr. Guzowski rushed forward with a broken brick in his hand.

"Get out of Poland, monsters!" he shouted, and threw the brick.

It struck one of the infantrymen in the shoulder. What happened next was like something out of a nightmare. The German commander pulled out a gun, aimed it and fired at Mr. Guzowski. Aniela screamed as her elderly Jewish neighbor fell down. A thin stream of blood trickled from his head onto the cobblestones.

Papa pulled her close and turned her head away from the hideous sight. But Aniela would never forget the look of shock on Mr. Guzowski's face as the bullet struck him.

"One less Jew in the world," the commander said, and all his men began to laugh. He spoke in Polish, as if he wanted to be sure everyone understood him.

"All right, then," he shouted. "You have work to do! Get this street cleaned up!"

"We don't need him to tell us that," Stefan growled.

"What about Mr. Guzowski, Papa?" Aniela whispered.

But Papa only shook his head. Aniela had never seen such a look of fear on his face before.

The soldiers moved to various places on the street. One of them stopped in front of the butcher shop and stared through the taped window as Aniela, Papa, and Stefan went back to work. His blue eyes were cold and hard. Aniela thought they looked very old for such a young face. She didn't think this German soldier could be older than seventeen, like Jadzia's brother.

An officer came and spoke to him. Then the soldier barked at them in broken Polish. "You have meat, no?"

"Old meat," Papa said. "Full of glass and splinters because of your bombs."

The soldier held up his gun. Aniela cried out in terror. But the officer pushed the gun back down again and snapped something at the soldier in German.

"Get the meat for us," the officer ordered in Polish. He gave Aniela a smile. "It is a shame to waste good food, isn't it?"

Aniela bowed her head, terrified.

"It's a shame to murder innocent people," Stefan mumbled under his breath.

Aniela was the only one who heard him. She gave him a frightened look as Papa dragged the trash bin out to the street. The Germans chattered with each other in their own language as they pulled dirty meat from the debris.

"Get me a box," the officer told Papa.

Without a word, Papa obeyed. They filled it with the meat and the officer carried it away.

"Go upstairs, Aniela," Papa insisted. "We don't yet know of the damage up there."

"Yes, Papa," Aniela said sadly.

She picked up Mama's photograph and held it close to her for strength. Then she climbed the stairs. She put her hand on the doorknob and held her breath, afraid of what lay beyond. But when she opened it, she was relieved to see that little damage had been done. Like Stefan's apartment, there were a few broken items. But nothing of value had been destroyed.

At least not this time, said a little voice inside of her.

"No, I won't listen!" Aniela cried. "There won't be a next time!"

She went into her room. The old dolls and books she kept stacked on her shelves had been knocked down. Slowly, she began to set them up again. She worked hard, trying to be strong. Papa had said the British and French would help them. Surely now that Warsaw had been invaded, they would send troops? Surely they would rescue the Polish people soon?

She picked up an old teddy bear. Papa had told her that Mama had bought it in America while visiting her sister in Chicago. She had been pregnant with Aniela at the time. Aniela had hugged and kissed it so much when she was little that it was missing a button eye and stuffing pushed through its worn seams.

Aniela began to cry. Not just quiet tears, but great, loud sobs that shook her whole body. She clutched Teddy close to her. Why had this happened? Who were these horrible Nazis that they just marched into a country and took charge? She thought of Mr. Guzowski, who had given her a piece of candy on her birthday. Why had the commander shot him? And why had Mr. Guzowski been so foolish to throw that brick?

"If you have an answer for me, God," she said out loud, "I'm listening."

But there was no answer. There was nothing to do but clean up, and hope this nightmare would be a short one.

Chapter Four

ON October 5th, Aniela and all the people of Warsaw saw the man who had brought them such misery. A great parade marched through Warsaw. There were Nazi troops and tanks, and trucks decorated with the flag of the Third Reich. And among them, Adolf Hitler himself. He stood in the front of a large car with an opened top. With one hand, he held the rim of the windshield. He thrust the other arm forward, his hands and fingers straight and stiff in a strange salute.

Aniela had to cling to Papa to keep from shuddering as he went by: How evil he looked! Beneath the brim of his cap, his eyes were cold and hard, like little pieces of stone. His mouth was set in a tight frown. Clearly, this was a madman, as Papa and Stefan had declared in secret. They did not dare speak such things out loud.

Mr. Guzowski had been only the first of many people of Warsaw who were shot for the slightest reasons. Even someone as young as Aniela could see that most of the Nazi's victims were those of higher education, called the Intelligentsia. She guessed the Nazis were afraid of anyone who could think and plan against them.

When the parade finally turned the corner, Papa led Aniela back into the butcher shop. It hardly was much of a shop now, with only a few pieces of meat. No Polish customers lined up for the chicken and sausage. The law now said the Germans came first in everything. Most of Papa's few customers were men in black-and-tan Nazi uniforms. Every other shop on the block had the same troubles, from the bakery to the shoe repair. The Germans had established a system of rationing now, with each family allowed only a certain amount of food a week.

"I hope that man goes away quickly, Papa," Aniela said. "I'm afraid of him."

"And well you should be, little one. He is a partner of the Devil. But don't you dare repeat such a thing outside," he warned.

"I know, Papa. I will keep it in my heart, in secret. Just like I keep my prayers."

Just then, the bell jingled and the shop door opened. Aniela turned slowly, because she did not want to face another Nazi officer. But, this time, she saw to her relief that it was Mrs. Ryzop from the dress shop. She led a small group of other neighbors and shopkeepers.

"I'm sorry," Papa said, "but there isn't enough to sell to all of you. Just a few oxtails and a bit of kielbasa. And Commander Himmel wants my only piece of beef."

"It isn't your meat we want, Max," Mrs. Ryzop said. She turned to Aniela and gave her a sad little smile. "It is Aniela's beautiful music. How we need it now, with our hearts so heavy!"

"Yes," added Mr. Kozmyk, the baker. "Play some Polish music for us, Aniela. Help us to forget that horrible parade of evil we just witnessed."

Aniela looked at her father. He nodded, and everyone walked into Stefan's apartment. Aniela had her piano teacher's permission to use the piano whenever she liked. Stefan himself was gone for the morning. Aniela had heard him whisper something to Papa about a meeting. He seemed to go to a lot of meetings now, but he refused to say a word about them to Aniela. She knew he wouldn't mind if visitors gathered in his little parlor. She sat down at the piano and sorted through the sheet music.

"Wait," Papa said. "We had better close the windows. If they hear her playing Polish music . . ."

He did not need to finish. No law against such music had been declared, but they all knew the sound of it would provoke Nazi anger. It was, after all, a show of defiance.

Aniela began to play. She played a sad Chopin tune, then "Fairwell to the Homeland," by another Polish composer named Michael Oginski. She opened up Stefan's copy of the *Songbook for Home Use*, written a century earlier by Stanislaus Moniuszko, and chose some of his happier tunes. Despite their sadness, the little group began to clap and sing along. Finally, Aniela played the Polish national anthem. Everyone sang it with her. When she finished, she turned to see tears streaming down everyone's faces. Even Papa's. He did not even bother to hide them now.

"We'd better go now," Mr. Kozmyk said. He had pulled the shade aside just a little to peek out at the street. "Someone is coming."

"Yes, we don't want to be seen in a group like this," Papa agreed. "Groups make the Nazis uneasy."

One by one, as they left, each adult thanked Aniela for her music. It had been a blessing in the midst of a terrible morning. Mrs. Ryzop hugged her tightly.

"Maybe now, when I go to sleep tonight," she said, "I will hear your music, and not see the face of that monster."

AS the weeks passed, Aniela saw many changes around her. The Polish people were soon stripped of all their rights. There were posters everywhere declaring new laws. One commanded that Polish people must always step aside when passing a German. They could not even speak their own language in public! There was nothing but static on Radio Poland now, and no daily newspaper. Polish theaters and restaurants were closed down. Even the cinema, where Aniela and her friends had sometimes watched American movies, was boarded up.

When Aniela woke up one morning, yellow and orange lights danced on her walls. She jumped from her bed and climbed onto her window seat. To her horror, Mr. Guzowski's bookshop across the street was on fire. Instead of a fire brigade working to put it out, Nazi soldiers stood guard with their rifles in hand and watched the building burn down. All week long, more fires flared up as the Nazis destroyed the bookshops and libraries.

The school still stood, and the children still met with their teachers for lessons. Parents were so worried about the children walking to school, with so many German soldiers about, that they took turns escorting them. Sometimes, Stefan would walk with Aniela, Jadzia, and Edith.

"I don't know what we will do when you go to the Army, Stefan," Aniela said. "I always feel so safe when you are with us."

"I can't go to the Army now," Stefan said. "It's forbidden. They posted another edict yesterday declaring that all young Polish men must join the German Army."

"I hate all these posters!" Jadzia cried.

"Jadzia, shh!" Edith hushed. She looked about frantically. "Someone bad might hear you!"

"I don't care," Jadzia said. "They are monsters and I hope they all die! I hate them. Mama cries and cries every night because we do not know what happened to my father and brother!"

She started to cry. Aniela and Edith put their arms around her.

"I don't know of my papa and brothers, either," Edith said softly.

There had been little word from the battlefront, but Aniela knew that the Polish soldiers who had not been killed were now prisoners of war. She felt almost guilty that she was the only one who still had her father here. It was only his bad leg that had kept him out of the Army.

"Are you going to join the Germans, Stefan?" she asked.

Stefan shook his head. "I'd rather die."

"But how will you resist? They are so strong, and so many!" Jadzia said.

Now Stefan smiled. It made him look as handsome as ever, and yet his eyes were very serious.

"I have my ways," he said. "I do have to register with them. If I don't, I will be arrested. But I won't put on their uniform or march with them!"

They had reached the school. To their dismay, they found a heavy chain and lock around the gate.

"What is this?" Aniela exclaimed.

There was yet another sign, nailed to the gatepost. This one declared the school closed, by order of Commander Himmel.

"First, they stop the bookshops and libraries," Stefan muttered. "And then the education of our young people. Do you know they've even started to change the names of our streets, to give them German names?"

"Why are they doing that?" Edith asked.

Stefan turned to stare down the street. From here they could see a troop of Nazi soldiers marching into the main part of town, a few blocks away.

"They want to erase the Polish people," he said quietly. "They want us to disappear from the face of the Earth."

"How can they do that?" Aniela asked. "How can they make so many of us just go away? It's impossible!"

Stefan put an arm around her shoulder. "We did not think they could defeat our Army, did we? We thought it would rain and their tanks would become bogged down in all our mud. But the rain did not come until too late, and our cavalry and infantry were no match for them."

"Papa says if other countries had helped us, we would have been all right," Aniela said with a frown.

"It might be so," Stefan agreed. "But we can't change things now. Come, let's go back home again. I'm sure your parents will all find a way for you children to have your education."

They did exactly that. Nobody, not even a man with Hitler's power, could stop the Polish people from keeping their dreams alive. Children met in small, secret groups and continued to learn their lessons. Different adults volunteered to take turns as teachers, even Stefan and Papa. At first, Aniela was terrified that a door would burst open and they would be arrested. But as the weeks passed, she began to relax. She hated all the new rules, and hated the Nazis who marched through her streets even more. But if she could keep on learning, and if she could continue her piano lessons, she would be as happy as possible.

The air grew colder and the leaves changed from green to brilliant reds, oranges, and yellows. People continued to work to clean up the rubble of the bombings, always under the careful eye of Nazi soldiers. Aniela was sad to learn that the president of Warsaw, Stefan Starzynski, had been arrested. More arrests followed, including some of Aniela's own neighbors.

"Why did they take Mrs. Ryzop and Mr. Sawicki away?" she asked Papa at dinner one night. She had done her best to make oxtail soup, with the few bits of meat and vegetables available. The portions were hardly enough to keep a growing girl alive, let alone satisfy a big man like Papa. She ate slowly to make it last.

"They were caught at a secret meeting," Papa said.

Aniela's hand clenched around her glass of water. A few months ago, it would have brimmed with cold, delicious milk. But there was only enough milk for breakfast now.

"Oh, Papa, Stefan goes to secret meetings, doesn't he? Please tell him to stop!"

"Stefan is a man of twenty-one," Papa replied. "I can't tell him what to do."

He took a piece of bread and mopped up the last drops of broth in his bowl.

"Aniela, you don't want him to give in to our enemies, do you?"

"I don't want him arrested," Aniela protested.

"We must take risks when we fight for our freedom, little one," Papa said. "If we back down like sheep, the Nazis will become more like wolves. All you can do is trust that Stefan will be careful. He is a smart man."

Aniela did not care how smart Stefan was. She wanted him safe, not smart! When she went to bed that night, she prayed as hard as she could that God and Mary and St. Hedwig and every other angel and saint would watch over Stefan.

A German soldier, so young he could almost be Aniela's age, entered the butcher shop one day and handed Max Kaminski a piece of paper. In broken Polish, he ordered that it be tacked up for the customers to read.

"What customers?" Papa asked. "I have so little to sell. There won't be many to read this."

Aniela held her breath. She watched the young German's mouth go thin and his shoulders stiffen. Papa stood at his full height, a good head taller than the boy. He was twice as big, too. The soldier seemed to realize this and relaxed a little. There was no point in trying to fight.

"Just do as you're told," he snapped. He thrust his arm up and forward and shouted: "Heil Hitler!"

Then he turned and left. Papa read the paper.

"Find a tack for me, Aniela," he said as he handed it to her.

"What is it, Papa?"

"They want a census," Papa said. "All Polish citizens are to register their names."

The next afternoon, Papa and Aniela joined other families in a long line outside Nazi headquarters. Children played games on the broken-up cobblestone street as the grownups talked quietly among themselves. Aniela, Edith and Jadzia huddled together as they watched. Aniela was close to the line, and noticed that each time a Nazi officer walked by, the adults would stop talking. Finally, Papa called her back to the line.

"Wait for me by Pulaski's statue," she told her friends.

"You mean by his feet," Jadzia said. "That's all that's left of him, you know."

Aniela nodded. A Nazi bomb had destroyed the statue.

Papa kept his arm around Aniela's shoulder. When they reached the front of the line, a man asked them questions. He had the lightest yellow hair and iciest blue eyes Aniela had ever seen. It was almost as if he were filled with snow. The questions were simple, but there was one that confused Aniela.

"Are you Jewish?"

Aniela looked up at Papa with a frown. He hugged her more tightly to keep her quiet.

"We are Roman Catholics," Papa answered.

The man noted this. There were a few more questions, and then he waved them away. Aniela and Papa joined the other girls at the broken statue. Jadzia's mother and Edith's mother were also there.

"I don't like this," said Mrs. Kolbe. "Why do they need our names? They are up to something!"

"And why did they ask if we are Jewish, Papa? What difference does it make?" Aniela asked.

"It makes a lot of difference to them," said Mrs. Lukowicz. "They hate us Jews. I fear for my children's safety."

Papa nodded. "As I do, too. But, Mrs. Lukowicz, this is not the place to discuss things like this. There are too many people about."

A look of fear passed over the Jewish woman's face. She yanked Edith close to her as if to protect her.

"I'll take my daughter home now," she said.

"Mama, can't I stay with Aniela and Jadzia?" Edith asked. "There was hardly any time to spend with them."

Mrs. Lukowicz looked so sad that Aniela thought she might burst into tears.

"What kind of world is this?" Edith's mother asked, "that we are afraid to let our children play?"

"Well, I, for one, refuse to live in fear!" Mrs. Kolbe declared. "Mr. Kaminski, will you stay with my daughter so she can play at your house?"

"Of course I will. I won't let the girls out of my sight," Papa assured her.

Now everyone turned to Mrs. Lukowicz. Edith had such a look of hope on her face that her mother had to give in. She nodded.

"All right, but only for an hour," she said. "And only because Mr. Kaminski will keep an eye on you."

So the three friends were able to play that afternoon. They styled each other's hair and talked about American movie stars and movies. Then the girls lit a candle and said prayers for Jadzia and Edith's fathers and brothers.

"I can't pray to your Blessed Virgin Mary," Edith said.

"But we can all talk to God," Aniela said.

Jadzia made a *hmmph* noise. "I'm not sure He listens."

"Jadzia!" Edith gasped.

Before Jadzia could reply, Papa knocked at the door. He poked his head inside and said that it was time for them to go home.

"You can start dinner, Aniela, while I escort your friends."

The three girls said good-bye and Aniela went into the kitchen. She wondered what kind of dinner she could make with just a tiny bit of kielbasa. There was still plenty of sauerkraut—cabbage was cheap. But now there was hardly any water to cook it. The bombs had contaminated the water supply and even that was strictly rationed. Finally, Aniela cut the kielbasa into thin slices. She fried these until they were just a little brown around the edges, then filled the skillet with the sauerkraut. She peeled three potatoes, cut them up and threw them on top. Then she put the lid on the skillet and turned to set the table.

When Papa came home, he told her she made a fine

meal. He acted as if it was a feast, but Aniela knew he was still hungry when they finished.

"I wonder what our cousins in America had to eat tonight?" she asked as she washed dishes.

"Nothing as fine as this, I'm sure," Papa said.

Aniela laughed. "You are only being kind, Papa. There was hardly any food on your plate."

"It won't fill me up to complain, though, will it?" Papa asked.

Aniela smiled at him. How she wished she could be as strong, and full of hope, as her father.

Chapter Five

EVERY November 1st, Aniela and her father always went to church to observe All Soul's Day. But St. Hedwig's had been boarded up, and Father Henryk had been arrested. Still, the Catholics of Warsaw prayed in the privacy of their homes. Every year before this, Aniela had prayed only for her mama. But now when she bowed her head, her mind was filled with many faces. She prayed that Father Henryk was safe. She prayed for Mrs. Ryzop, who had been executed shortly after her arrest. In her mind, the woman stood next to Mr. Guzowski in a rubble-filled lot. They were surrounded by dozens of other sad spirits, lives that had been cut off by Nazi terror.

She saw Polish soldiers, too, with faces she did not know. But she saw Jadzia's and Edith's fathers and brothers among them. She hoped hard that it was only a trick of her mind, and that they hadn't been killed in battle. She prayed for all the soldiers. She prayed for those who had died of the diseases that had spread after the bombings, and for those who had died of hunger because food and water were so scarce.

Each evening, when it became too dark to see, Aniela lit candles through the apartment. But tonight, Papa stopped her before she lit the two tall white ones they kept on the mantel.

"There is to be a vigil tonight," Papa said. "We are all going to carry candles to remember those who have died."

"Papa, will the Germans allow it?"

"I have been told that Commander Himmel will not stop us," Papa said. "But we must walk in peace and not provoke their anger."

Aniela could hardly believe how many people crowded the main avenue. A thousand candles lit up the night as the parade moved to the cemetery. There were almost as many lights as there were tears! All around her, she saw women in black veils. They were mothers who had lost sons and wives who were now widows. Men bowed their heads and even the smallest children were solemn. Each one set a candle down on a gravesite. Some of her neighbors set their own candles along the path that led through the graveyard. These were for the soldiers who had never returned home.

"Please, God," she whispered, "let Jadzia's and

Edith's fathers and brothers come back. And don't let the Germans take Stefan!"

ONE November morning, Aniela left her house to attend class. These little school sessions were never held in the same place two days in a row, and there were never more than four or five children present. Each class was taught by a different grownup who volunteered a few hours of time. It was the safest way to keep the children's education secret from the Gestapo, the Nazi secret police. Until the morning of each class, only the parents knew where it would be held. Today, Papa instructed Stefan to escort the girls to Maryla Sokop's house. Maryla was one of their classmates, and her mother would teach them today.

They met Jadzia first. She was bundled up in a sweater and coat and gloves.

"You look as if it's already January," Stefan teased.

"I'm freezing!" Jadzia shuddered. "We had no heat in the house last night. We ran out of kerosene and there is none to be had anywhere."

"We're using carbide now," Aniela said. "Papa says it's easy to find, and it's cheap."

Jadzia declared, "I don't care what we use, as long as I am warm in my bed tonight!"

They reached Edith's house. The Lukowicz family lived in a pretty brick home surrounded by a small yard. The bombing in September had destroyed Mrs. Lukowicz's roses and had torn the fence out of the ground. The bushes lay in a dry and brown pile now. The broken fence was thrown on top of the woodpile.

Edith opened the door, dressed in a green coat that was a little too big for her. It was a hand-me-down from her bigger sister. At once, Aniela saw the white armband, with blue stripes and a blue Star of David, wrapped around her friend's upper arm.

"What is that for?" she asked.

"Someone brought it to our house this morning," Edith said. "All Jews have to wear them."

"Why?" Jadzia asked.

Edith shrugged. "I don't know. But the man said if we did not wear them, we would be arrested. They know who all the Jews are, after that day we registered our names."

Aniela moved closer to Stefan. He put his arm around her.

"I don't like this, Stefan. It scares me! What do these Nazis have in mind?"

"I can't say," Stefan said quietly. "Come now, girls. I want to get you safely to Maryla's house."

Now Aniela saw the blue-and-white armbands everywhere. Even the youngest children wore them. She could hardly concentrate on her lessons for worry. What was going to happen to Edith and her family?

THERE was so much sorrow around her that Aniela wasn't certain God heard anyone's prayers. But one day, Edith ran into the butcher shop with a big grin on her face. She grabbed Aniela and danced around with her. Aniela laughed even though she did not understand her friend's joy.

"Edith! Why are you so happy today?"

"Papa is alive!" Edith cried. "Papa and my brothers!"

Now Aniela's father came out from behind the counter. He put two big hands on Edith's thin shoulders.

"What are you talking about?" he asked with concern in his eyes. "How did you find out?"

"Mama got a letter," Edith explained. "Someone delivered it to her late last night. She told me the news when I woke up!"

Just then, the shop door opened and a German soldier entered. Papa leaned close to Edith.

"Say nothing more," he commanded in a whisper.

Edith frowned at Aniela's father. Aniela wondered why Papa wanted her friend to be silent.

"Let's go upstairs," she said.

When they were in her bedroom, they sat in Aniela's window seat. Aniela hugged her friend tight. "I'm so happy for you. When will your father and brothers come home?"

"I don't know," Edith said. "Mama said the man who delivered the letter told her that all anyone knew is that Papa and my brothers are alive and well. No one knows exactly where they are. He said it had been a risk to bring the letter to Mama, and that she should burn it at once."

"Then maybe they aren't in a Nazi prison?" Aniela asked hopefully.

"I don't think so," said Edith.

Papa knocked at the door and entered. He knelt down in front of the girls.

"Edith, it was a secret letter, wasn't it?" he asked.

"Yes, sir," replied Edith. "The man told Mama to burn it."

"Then he didn't want anyone to know your father and brothers are alive," Papa said. "Very few people get word of their men these days. If your Mama got a letter, then your father and brothers must be in a secret place. The letter was smuggled through the country. For their safety, you must not speak of them as if they are alive."

"But how can I hide my joy?"

"You must," Papa insisted. "If the Nazis hear you, they will question your family to learn how you found out about your father and brothers. It can only mean disaster!"

Edith bowed her head.

"I hate these Nazis with all my heart," she said. "They take away all my happiness."

"But you only have to show a sad face to the Germans," Aniela said. "Here in my room, you can celebrate!"

"Yes, Aniela is right," Papa said. "And I have something for you."

He left the room and came back with two little cakes. Aniela gasped.

"Papa! Where did you find those?"

"I traded a little sausage, and never mind with who. We have to get things secretly these days, like Edith's letter. The cakes were to be our dessert tonight, for we haven't had sweets in so long. But I'll give them to you girls instead. You can eat them and honor Edith's wonderful news!"

Aniela and Edith both gave Papa a kiss. He left them to tend to his shop downstairs. The girls ate slowly, savoring each bite of the sweet little cakes. After weeks of nothing but potatoes, sauerkraut, and a little bread, the cakes tasted like ambrosia.

"Mmmm." Edith sighed. "This is so good!"

"I'm going to make mine last as long as possible," Aniela said. "I don't know when we'll ever have cakes again."

Edith licked icing from her finger. "When the war is over, and the Nazis go away, I'm going to have the biggest party ever. I'm going to invite everyone in Warsaw, and have cake and ice cream and sweets for everyone!"

"And plenty of coal to keep us warm," Aniela added with a grin.

"And milk!"

"And meat!"

"But not on the same plate," Edith said. "It would be a kosher party, of course."

Aniela giggled. "It's almost time for your special holiday, isn't it? Hanukkah?"

"Yes, and if we are lucky," Edith said, "Papa and my brothers will be home with us then."

Now Aniela looked out the window. She saw a couple approach a German soldier. As they neared, the soldier stopped. They stared at each other for a moment, then the couple stepped into the gutter and let the soldier pass. Aniela thought of Jadzia just then. Stepping aside for Germans was one of the rules Jadzia hated so much.

"Poor Jadzia," Aniela murmured. "I hope she gets the same good news about her father and brother as you have."

"I'll keep praying for her family," Edith said.

"I pray every night," Aniela told her. "God finally listened to me and brought you this good news. Now I hope he does the same for our Jadzia!"

Edith popped the last bite of cake into her mouth, then leaned forward to hug Aniela.

"Thank you, Aniela," she said. "Thank you for your prayers, and for being my best friend!"

"We'll be friends forever!" Aniela vowed.

The two girls hugged. They could not know, in their moment of great happiness, that it was the last time they would ever see each other.

Chapter Six

WHEN Aniela looked out her window the next morning, a curtain of falling snow hid the pointed roof of St. Hedwig's church. Everything outside was covered in white, and soft flakes fell steadily from the sky above. It made everything so hushed and pure that, for a few moments, Aniela could almost believe she was in another world. Wouldn't it be wonderful if that were true? It would be nice to wake up in another world, far away from Nazis and guns and cruel new laws.

It was chilly in her room. Aniela found a warm sweater, a wool skirt, and wool stockings in her bureau. After she dressed, she went into the kitchen to make breakfast. Papa sat at the table reading a book, one of the few the Nazis had not confiscated. It was so old the spine was torn and the front cover hung at an angle. But Papa did not have the newspaper he used to read before the Germans took over. There were no more newspapers, although once in a while someone smuggled a sheet of news into the city. Papa had read such a sheet yesterday, but had already passed it on to a neighbor.

"Good morning, Papa," she said, and kissed his rough cheek.

"Good morning, Aniela. What do you think of this snow, so early in December?"

"It's beautiful," Aniela said.

"Yes," Papa said and looked out the window. "At least it is one thing they can't take away from us . . . the work of God's hands."

Aniela went to the stove. Papa had always liked a strong cup of coffee, but there was hardly any coffee available now. Most of it, Stefan had told her, went to the German soldiers. So the coffee she made for Papa was weak, without even a spoonful of sugar to give it more flavor. But Papa never complained about it. She made hot cakes, and wished that there was syrup and butter for them. But then she thought of people who might not even have this much and decided she would be like Papa and keep silent.

"Well, there certainly won't be any school for you today," Papa said.

"Can I go see Jadzia and Edith?" Aniela asked him. "I'd like to build a snowman in the lot down the street."

"When the snow lets up a bit," Papa promised.

But the snow did not stop for the rest of the day. Aniela tried to call her friends from the telephone in the butcher shop, but the lines were down because of the storm. She spent the morning reading and drawing. In the early afternoon, she went downstairs for her piano lesson.

"Can we play some Christmas carols today?" Aniela asked Stefan eagerly.

"I think that's a fine idea." Stefan smiled. "After all, the snow makes Christmas seem right around the corner, doesn't it?"

"It's just a few weeks away," Aniela said. "But I wonder what it will be like this year, with everything so different."

Stefan opened a cabinet and found a big, fat music book full of carols. He opened to "Cantique de Noel" and set it on the music stand.

"This is my favorite of all," Aniela said. She began to play the beautiful song that most everyone called "O Holy Night." The door that led from the parlor into the butcher shop was open, and she heard customers go in and out. These days, they came more for conversation with Papa than to buy meat. Papa's display cases were almost empty. As Aniela finished the song, Mr. Kozmyk, the baker, poked his head into the doorway.

"Very beautiful, young lady," he praised. "Can you bring that piano to the bakery and play for my customers?"

Aniela laughed to imagine pushing the big upright

piano down the snow-covered street. What would the Nazi soldiers think of that?

"You can always send them down here to listen," Stefan replied.

The bell over Papa's door jingled, and everyone's smile faded at once to see Commander Himmel. He strode by Papa as if he didn't even see him.

"Stefan Olczak?" he asked.

"That is my name," Stefan said.

The commander did not answer him right away. He looked at Aniela. His eyes were so dark that she had to grasp the edges of the piano bench to keep from shuddering. When he walked closer to her, and stretched out his arm, she thought she might scream. But he only reached for the music book and picked it up. He flipped through the pages until he found something, then set it down again. It was an old German tune, "O, Tannenbaum."

"Play this," he said in an abrupt way that meant she could not protest. "And loudly."

Aniela looked at Stefan, who gave her a very slight nod of encouragement. Then she turned to look at the doorway. Mr. Kozmyk had slipped away, but Papa watched her carefully as he cut up a scrawny chicken on his counter. She took in a deep breath and began to play. She used the pedals much more than usual, and pressed the keys hard. Would that be loud enough for the commander?

She heard him talking with Stefan, but could not understand their German words. It was only their tones that told her they were having an argument. Finally, the song came to an end. Commander Himmel snapped his fingers at her, and she began to play again. She went through it three times before he finally told her to stop.

"Beautiful playing," he said. "I might have you play for my officers at my Christmas dinner."

He sung the song in his native German as he left the shop. Aniela had to shake out her fingers, for the strong playing had made the backs of her hands ache.

"What did he want, Stefan?"

"Never mind," Stefan said. He no longer wore a pleasant expression, but frowned as if he'd just heard terrible news. "It isn't anything for you to worry about. I think that's enough lessons for today, Aniela. Why don't you go on upstairs?"

"I wish I could see my friends today," she pouted. "But Papa says it isn't safe to walk outside in this weather."

Now Stefan did smile, but the smile didn't reach his eyes. Aniela knew he was only trying to be cheerful for her.

"I'm sure the snow will let up by tonight," he said, "and you'll meet with your friends in the morning."

Aniela left the apartment. Papa was telling a customer how best to stretch a small piece of liver to feed six people, and did not even see her. She trudged upstairs, her hands still aching and her shoes feeling very heavy. She kicked them off when she climbed into her window seat to gaze out at the white world below. It looked like a Christmas card.

That gave her an idea. She went to her little desk and found paper, scissors, and colored pencils. She would decorate the apartment for Christmas, since Papa had been too worried; and too busy to do so. She found some string in the kitchen drawer and borrowed a few of Papa's hangers. For the next hour, she created *pajaki*, mobiles that would help decorate the apartment for Christmas. She hung them all around the kitchen and living room. When Papa came in, he laughed out loud.

"It surely does look like Christmas in here, Aniela," he said.

"Do you like them, Papa?" Aniela asked anxiously. "They aren't all glittery and pretty. And they aren't as nice as a tree."

Papa hugged her. "They are wonderful, Aniela. Just wonderful."

"I wish we could bring Mama's crèche up here." Aniela sighed.

"I know," Papa said. "But I'm afraid to put it out. Should anyone bad come up here, they would destroy it."

Aniela thought of her mother's manger scene, hidden away so carefully in the cellar with the china and crystal. Would they be able to bring them out by next year?

When the weather finally cleared, Aniela pulled on

her boots and heavy coat and went out to meet with her friends. As always, Papa said she could not go alone.

"It isn't safe," Papa said. "And you have to take a longer walk to get to the inn now, don't you?"

"Yes, Papa."

Gestapo headquarters had been set up on one of the streets Aniela used in her walk to the inn where Jadzia lived. Now she took a roundabout way to avoid it, always fearful that one of the Nazis would confront her.

"Can you walk with me, Papa?" she asked.

"My leg is acting up, little one." Papa shook his head regretfully. "It's this snow."

Aniela frowned. It was the Nazis, not the snow, that made Papa ache. There wasn't enough heat in the apartment, and they had run out of his pain medicine during the storm. The nearest pharmacy had been destroyed in the bombing, and medicine was hard to get.

Just then, Stefan came from his room behind the shop. He wore a heavy coat and kept one hand deep in his left pocket.

"Stefan, would you walk with me to Jadzia's home?" Aniela asked.

"Of course," Stefan replied. "What else is there for me to do, with the library and bookshop gone and the college closed?"

"Thank you, Stefan," Papa said. "I know my daughter is safe with you."

As they walked down the street, Stefan often

looked back over his shoulder. Aniela sensed that he was nervous about something.

"Are you all right?" she whispered.

"Shh," he hushed, and tilted his head forward just a little.

Aniela looked and saw two German soldiers approaching them. She held her breath. But they were too busy talking to each other to really notice them. Stefan touched her arm and they moved into the gutter (Like dogs, Aniela thought) to let the soldiers go by them. Once they turned the corner to an empty street, though, Stefan leaned close to her.

"I have a book," he whispered. "A few friends from the University are meeting to read today."

He patted it against his thigh. Aniela realized there was a hole in his pocket, and his hand reached down through it.

"What book, Stefan?" Aniela asked him.

"Shakespeare's play *Hamlet*," said Stefan. "Perhaps we can't see it at the theater now, but we can still read it."

Aniela slipped a little on some ice. Stefan grabbed her with his free arm. When she was steady, she spoke.

"You have a secret school," she marveled, "just like the children."

"That's right, Aniela," Stefan said. "You see, they can't stop us completely, can they?"

Aniela had to laugh at that. No, the Nazis weren't as smart as they thought they were!

They reached Jadzia's building. Jadzia stood on

the steps of the inn with a bucketful of icicles in one hand. When she saw Aniela, she smiled and put the bucket down.

"Hello, Aniela!" she called, her voice softened by the drifts of snow that had blown up against the stone buildings. "Hello, Stefan!"

"Good morning, Jadzia," said Stefan. He held her hand and helped her climb over a mountain of snow.

"I'm so glad you're here," Jadzia said. "I've been so bored!"

"Can you go to Edith's house with me?" Aniela asked.

"Let me tell Mama," Jadzia said. She picked up her bucket again. "We melt the icicles for water for our tenants, you know."

She went inside. As they waited, Aniela and Stefan heard the familiar stomping of boots from around the corner. She looked at Stefan, hoping his warm smile would help her be brave if the Nazis stopped them. But Stefan was gone.

Aniela swung in a full circle. Panic began to rise inside of her. Why had Stefan disappeared?

"Stefan, where are you?"

Aniela was about to slip inside the lobby of the inn when Stefan appeared again. This time he had both hands out of his coat. She frowned at him.

"Stefan, where . . . ?"

He held a finger to his lips and nodded a little toward the alley between the inn and the boarded-up restaurant next door. Before Aniela could say a word, two

Nazi soldiers marched toward them. Unlike the pair that had been too busy to bother with them earlier, these men stopped and stared hard.

"What are you doing out here?" said one, in a voice so loud even the blanket of snow on the sidewalk did not muffle it.

"We are waiting for a friend," Stefan said. "I'm escorting these girls to a friend's house. Something that would not be necessary if the streets were safe for children."

The first Nazi leaned closer to him. He peered into Stefan's glasses, as if he could see through his eyes and tell if he lied.

"Listen to this, Rolf," he said to his partner. "The Polish swine has nothing better to do than play with little girls!"

Rolf laughed. "Look how weak and skinny he is, Hans! Where is your doll, Polack?"

Hans gave Stefan a poke, which made him stumble a little.

"Did you sign up for the Army, Polack?"

When Stefan answered, his words were very careful and steady. Aniela knew he burned inside with hatred.

"Yes, I did," Stefan said. "It is the law, is it not?"

He asked this question in a way that almost seemed to say the Nazis might be too stupid to know their own laws. Aniela held her breath and prayed that the Nazi would let it pass. But Hans swung out an arm and backhanded Stefan across the face.

"Shut your mouth." He sneered, "You are lucky I have other orders to follow today, or you would be on that sidewalk with a bullet through your head."

Now Aniela couldn't help a cry of horror. The Nazi Rolf looked at her, and then he smiled. There was a look of sympathy on his face, but it did not fill his eyes. He put an arm around her shoulders and roughly pulled her close to him.

"Such a pretty girl should not be afraid of us," he said.

"Such a pretty girl should not be Polish," added Hans.

"Please," Aniela whispered. Her stomach had shrunk into a tight little ball.

Now Rolf pushed her roughly away. He said something to Hans in German. Hans spit at Stefan, then the two walked away without another word.

Aniela turned to Stefan and saw that his lip had been split.

"Oh, Stefan!" she cried. "You're hurt!"

"I'm all right," he breathed. "I only thank God they're gone and that you weren't harmed."

He reached under his coat, into a pocket of his trousers, and pulled out a handkerchief. Filling it with snow, he held it to his swelling lip.

Jadzia came out then.

"Oh, Aniela!" she cried. "It is a good thing Mama always looks out on the street before I go outside! We saw those Nazis! Are you all right, Stefan? Mama says come inside if you want."

"I'm just fine, really," Stefan said, and managed a smile that Aniela knew was only there for the girls' benefit.

"Well, let's go to Edith's house now," Aniela said, "before those awful men come back."

"Edith's house," Stefan said in a quiet voice, almost as if he didn't understand the words.

"Yes, we want to see our friend, of course," Aniela reminded him.

"I didn't . . ." Stefan hesitated. "I didn't realize that. All right, then. Let's go."

Aniela wondered why he sounded so strange. She and Jadzia always saw Edith. Then she decided he probably didn't want to face any more Nazis. He was probably nervous about that.

With the girls close behind him, Stefan went into the alley and opened up a trash can. His book, wrapped in brown paper that had once been a flour sack, lay on top of the garbage. He tucked it back down through his torn pocket again.

They walked in silence. Aniela's terror gave way to anger. Those men had no right to treat Stefan that way! He did nothing to provoke that. No, they had only done it to be spiteful. She wondered what kind of mothers they had when they were little, to bring up such hateful, horrible sons.

Edith's little house was only a block away. The first thing Aniela noticed was that the snow had not been shoveled from the sidewalk that led to the front door. Then she saw that all the window shades were drawn.

Mrs. Lukowicz loved the sunshine, and kept her shades and curtains opened until sundown each night. New black clouds of fear began to gather inside Aniela.

"Someone must be sick," she said, and hurried to the front door.

"Aniela, wait," Stefan called.

Aniela began to pound on the door. After a long time, when no one answered, she turned to Stefan and Jadzia. Jadzia's eyes were huge and shiny with tears.

"Something is wrong, Aniela," she whispered. "Where are Edith and her mother and sisters so early in the morning?"

Aniela looked at Stefan. There was something strange about his expression, as if he was hiding a secret. He did not meet her eyes.

"Stefan, do you know something?" she asked. "Where is my friend? Where is her family?"

Stefan took in a deep breath. When he let it out, it made a cloud in front of his face. Then he looked all around. The street was deserted, except for two dogs fighting over a bone and a few birds scavenging through the snow. Still, he spoke in a very, very quiet voice.

"Listen to me, you two," he said. "I am going to tell you something, and you must not ever, ever repeat it. Do you understand? It means your friend's life."

Both girls nodded eagerly. Stefan looked around again. Aniela knew he was making very certain they were alone. What secret could he have to tell them, she wondered, that made him so terribly anxious?

Chapter Seven

"DO you remember the note that came to Edith's mother?" Stefan asked.

"Yes, Stefan," Aniela said.

"She told me about it, too," Jadzia said.

"It was one of my . . . friends . . . who made the delivery," Stefan told them. "You see, many of us have been working to help free our people."

"The Polish Underground?" Aniela asked excitedly. "You are a member of The Polish Underground?"

Papa had told her about a secret group of people who worked hard to help their fellow countrymen.

"Yes, but you must pretend you never heard me say that," Stefan replied.

"That is why you went to so many meetings?" Aniela asked.

Stefan nodded. "Say no more about it now, Aniela. I will only tell you a little to ease your mind. Edith and her family are safe. We have heard that there is to be trouble, very bad trouble, for the Jews soon. For that reason, I worked to get the Lukowicz family out of Warsaw, perhaps even out of Poland."

"To where?" Aniela asked, her voice a little shrill.

"Never ask that," Stefan ordered sternly. "You only need to know that people are working to keep them—and others—safe. They will make their way to . . . to the place where they will meet with Edith's father and brothers."

Suddenly, Jadzia began to cry.

"I don't know about my father and brother," she blurted out. "And now I don't know about Edith!"

"Hush, Jadzia," Aniela murmured. "I'm sure you will hear from them one day; soon."

Jadzia blinked her tears away and looked at Stefan. "Can you find out about them, Stefan?"

"I'll do what I can," Stefan said, but his voice told her it was not a promise.

He looked up and down the street again. A man who had come out of the house next door stared at them as he shoveled snow. Stefan put his arms around the girls' shoulders and steered them away.

"We'd better get going," he said. "There are spies everywhere now, traitors willing to turn against their fellow countrymen."

When they entered the next street, they saw the same two Nazis who had attacked Stefan. They decided to take a roundabout way back to the butcher shop, and crossed through the park. The pathways had been shoveled. But all around them, snow rolled like white icing over the hilly ground. The tree branches bent low under the weight of the snow, and the melting drops looked like crystals in the sunlight.

"It's so beautiful," Aniela said, "like a fairyland. You could almost forget everything here, couldn't you?"

"Yes, for a moment," Stefan agreed. "Except that these walks were shoveled under the threat of Nazi guns."

"Oh, how awful," Jadzia said. "Why do they have to threaten us? We would have done the work on our own!"

They walked a little farther along the path. Now they saw something that made Jadzia gasp and Aniela turn her face into Stefan's coat. The snow had been disturbed near a copse of bare oak trees, and there was no denying what the shape imprinted in the white was that of a body. All around were splotches of red. Aniela realized someone had been executed here.

"That's blood, isn't it?" Jadzia whispered.

"I'm afraid it is," Stefan whispered. "Come on, we have to hurry. I don't like being out like this, not with you girls."

As they rushed home, Aniela's mind was full of thoughts. Would she ever see Edith again? Would her friend really be safe? Who had been shot back there in the park; and why? *Why?*

WHEN Aniela tried to tell Papa that Edith was safe, Papa shook his head and whispered that she must not say a word about her friend. Aniela understood that this was not only for Edith's safety, but for Stefan's. She had to pretend she did not know a thing about her friend. But nothing could stop her from keeping Edith in her heart.

Over the next days, there were more troubles for the Polish people. Aniela heard of citizens being dragged from their homes and shot in the streets. The Nazis seemed to be everywhere, dirtying the snow with their big, black boots and dirtying the air with their foul, cruel taunts. Aniela saw that the Jews took most of their abuse, but nasty words and abuse were also thrown at Christians. Papa told her, in a very quiet voice, that Hitler wanted to drive out all religion and make himself everyone's "God." He was definitely insane, Aniela thought. But what kind of madmen followed someone like that? Surely he couldn't have fooled all the German people! No matter what happened, Aniela had to believe there were still some good people in Poland's enemy country. And they were probably as scared to speak out as the Polish people were.

It was hard to find time for piano lessons now, although Aniela sat down and played as often as possible. Customers who came to talk with Papa kept guard, and warned her to stop playing whenever they saw a Nazi approach. One day, about a week after Edith's family left, Commander Himmel saw her leaving Stefan's apartment.

"No piano today, *liebling*?" he asked. He ran a finger down her cheek.

Aniela wanted to shudder with revulsion at his touch, but she knew that would cause trouble, so she bit her lip. She also hated the way he used that German endearment, a word that meant "sweetheart," for she knew he did not mean it.

"No, sir," she said. She kept her voice cold, but just respectful enough to keep the commander happy.

"Well, Christmas is but a week away," he said. "I'm still thinking about having you play at my party."

"Yes, sir," Aniela said. "May I go now?"

Himmel waved a hand at her, like a king dismissing a subject. Aniela had to restrain herself to keep from running up the stairs. Surely, Papa wouldn't let her go to that man's home and play the piano for those awful Nazis? The very thought terrified her so much that when she entered the apartment she went right to a statue of the Blessed Mother and fell to her knees.

"Please, Mother Mary," she begged, "please, please don't let them make me do that!"

She heard the apartment door open again. Papa had entered, and had a very worried look on his face. Aniela ran to hug him.

"Papa, I'm so scared," she cried. "I don't want to play for those terrible men!"

"You won't have to, I promise you, Aniela." Papa patted her back.

"But how can you stop it?"

Papa pulled away and took her chin in his big hand. There was a smile on his face that Aniela found very comforting.

"I have my ways," he said. "Do not worry about it."

"You talk like Stefan, Papa," Aniela said in a soft voice. "Please, please don't do anything dangerous for my sake!"

"Oh, little one," Papa said, "who else do I have to live for but you?"

"I love you, Papa," Aniela said, and hugged him again.

Now Papa clapped his hands together. "I'm hungry, Aniela. Let us see what feast you can cook with pig knuckles and onions!"

"Ugh!" Aniela grimaced.

She hated pig knuckles, but who could turn away even the worst food in these times? She did the best she could with them, but they still tasted awful to her. Once again, she reminded herself that others would give anything to have even this for dinner.

Papa had obtained another underground newspaper and read it while Aniela cleaned the kitchen. She thought about Papa's promise that she would not have to play for the Nazis. He seemed so sure of that, but who could be sure of anything these days? Later, in bed, she said more prayers for herself, her papa, and her country. Before she blessed herself, she added a quick plea for Stefan's safety.

Aniela had a nightmare that night. She dreamed

that she was playing Mama's white grand piano, but the audience was filled with Nazi officers and enlisted men. And who should walk on the stage but the man of everyone's nightmares, Adolf Hitler. Shouts of "Sieg Heil!" filled the room as the führer took a gun from his pocket and aimed at someone who stood in the wings. Aniela could not stop playing, even as she saw Papa fall to the floor.

She jerked awake to a room flooded with moonlight. She heard another gunshot, but wasn't sure if it was real, or still part of a dream. And then she heard shouting, in German, from the street below. Aniela jumped out of bed and ran to her window seat. She could see a group of uniformed men with a civilian. When he turned, the moonlight reflected off his glasses. Stefan!

She fumbled with the latch, but it was frozen tight. One of the Nazis fired his pistol at Stefan's feet, making him jump back. He stumbled over the pile of rubble that had been Mr. Guzowski's bookstore. Another Nazi kicked him hard, and his glasses flew from his head. They shouted words that Aniela could not hear. She worked harder to open the window. She wanted to shout at them, to make them go away!

Suddenly, Papa was yanking her back from the window seat.

"Papa!" she screamed, startled.

"Stay away from that window!" Papa yelled. "Don't let them see you watching!"

"But Papa, they're going to kill Stefan!"

"And they'll kill you, too, if they see you!" he said. "Get back into bed, and stay there. No matter what happens, no matter what you hear downstairs, you pretend you are asleep!"

"But Papa . . ." Aniela suddenly felt more afraid than she ever had in her life.

"If you want to see the morning, you'll obey me without question. Please, Aniela! No argument!"

Aniela climbed back into her bed and pulled her grandmother's quilt over her head. She shook so violently that the bed actually creaked beneath her. She prayed as hard as she could, tears streaming down her face. It seemed that hours had gone by before Papa came back again.

"They have gone. Go back to sleep now."

"What about Stefan, Papa?"

"You must forget about him," Papa insisted. "You must never mention his name again."

Without another word, he closed the door. Aniela thought she would never fall asleep again, but the next thing she knew it was morning. She had to drag herself from the bed, for the apartment was icy cold. Papa would send her to wait on line for coal, she supposed, unless he could get carbide from someone.

Papa had left a note on the kitchen table, saying he was already down in the shop. There was a little bit of oatmeal for breakfast, but Aniela wasn't hungry. She went downstairs to see about Stefan. Papa did not notice her when she walked into her piano teacher's apartment.

The piano was gone! There was nothing left of it but four round holes where its legs had dug into the old carpeting. Aniela looked around and saw that many of Stefan's other things were gone, too. She hurried back outside.

"Papa, where are Stefan's things?" she asked.

"I told you not to speak of him, Aniela," he said.

Aniela thought she might cry again, for she had never seen Papa so stern. He looked at her, and his expression softened.

"They came and confiscated his belongings early this morning," he said. "That is why I am already downstairs. I tried to tell Commander Himmel the piano belonged to us, but he would not listen."

"Do you know what happened to Stefan?"

Papa sighed. "He was arrested, Aniela. And it is only by the grace of God that I was not taken, too. I heard Stefan insist several times that we were not involved in anything he'd done."

"He didn't do anything, Papa!"

"He helped some Jewish people," he said. "In their minds, that's a crime. Aniela, please listen. You are so young to have to face these things. But I ask you to be an adult today. Hold your head high and pretend nothing happened. For if you don't, they will become suspicious of us!"

Aniela took a deep breath and squared her shoulders. She really wanted to crawl away, perhaps to hide down in the cellar among the boxes filled with Mama's good china and crystal. But she knew Papa was right.

"You have a class today at Jadzia's house," he said. "I can't walk you there, but I want you to go. It's important you do everything in the same way as always."

"What if I see Nazis, Papa?"

"You must be sure to see them first," he said. "Hide until they pass by. Now, hurry, or you'll be late."

He kissed her, then went to look at his ledger book. Aniela saw that there were only a few marks on the page. Just a few months ago, every line would have been filled to record a transaction.

She had never felt less like going to school. Her heart was very heavy, and it was all she could do not to cry when she thought of Stefan. She had heard terrible rumors about how the Germans treated their prisoners. What would they do to Stefan? Would they torture him to learn everything he knew about The Polish Underground?

Twice, Aniela had to duck behind a tree until German soldiers had turned a corner. She was grateful that the inn where Jadzia lived was close by. A few tenants turned to look at her with dull eyes when she entered the lobby and stomped the snow off her boots. Jadzia's oldest sister was behind the desk. She gave Aniela a little nod in greeting, but said nothing. Aniela climbed to the top floor, where Mrs. Kolbe and Jadzia waited with two neighborhood boys. Jadzia's youngest brother played in a corner with a little wooden truck, and her baby sister slept in a small wooden cradle near the hearth. There was only a small fire, perhaps fueled by wood taken from abandoned buildings.

"They took Stefan away last night," she whispered to Jadzia as she took off her coat.

"No!"

"I'm not allowed to talk about it," Aniela said. "Papa says we are in danger."

"Poor Stefan," Jadzia said with a shake of her head. "Poor Aniela!"

Mrs. Kolbe had laid out paper and pencils. No child dared to carry books through the city these days. Mrs. Kolbe taught them a lesson in math, and then in Polish history. Aniela thought of the laws that had closed Polish schools, forbade the Polish language, and any other signs of Polish patriotism. Stefan would want her to learn all she could about her country, in spite of the Nazis.

"I will learn all that I can, Stefan!" she thought as Jadzia read a passage from an ancient textbook. "I will never stop learning about my country. And one day, I will find a way to play piano again!"

She would dedicate her efforts to her beloved piano teacher. Perhaps then she might be able to go on without him.

Chapter Eight

"ANIELA?"

Aniela heard Papa's voice in a pleasant dream about a festival, where she danced a polka in traditional costume. Multicolored ribbons flew from her hair as she spun around with Stefan as her partner.

"Wake up, little one!"

The dream vanished and Aniela opened her eyes. Papa held a kerosene lamp. It was still dark outside, and wind rattled her window.

"Papa? Why are you up so early?"

"We have to catch a train," he said.

"A train?"

Now Aniela was fully awake. She pushed her quilt aside and sat up. It was cold in her room, and she shivered. Papa found her robe and put it over her shoulders.

"You have time for a small breakfast," he said. "I've already cooked some sausages for you, and there is bread from last night."

He left the room. Completely confused, Aniela pushed her arms through the sleeves of her robe and hurried, barefoot, into the kitchen. Papa had set a place for her. She sat down and began to eat, even though she was not at all hungry.

"Papa, what is happening?" she asked.

"I have train tickets to Koszalin," Papa explained. "They arrived late last night, after you fell asleep. But the train leaves the Warsaw station very early, and we must be on it. If we aren't, there will be no chance for us."

"No chance for us? Papa, I don't understand. Why do we have to go to Koszalin?"

"To take a ferry to Sweden," Papa said.

Aniela almost choked on a piece of sausage.

"Sweden! Why are we going to Sweden?"

"Aniela, you must not ask so many questions. Things have changed. It isn't safe for you in Warsaw. I want to get you out of here. Now, listen to me."

Aniela took a sip of milk and stared at her father. This was all so strange and sudden that she wondered if she was still in a dream.

"If anyone asks you where you are going," Papa said, "it is to visit a sick aunt in Sweden. She is your mother's sister."

"Mama had a sister?" Aniela was surprised to hear that, for Papa had never said a word about an aunt in Sweden.

Papa shook his head. "No, little one. There is no aunt. But it is the story you must tell, for we have to have a reason to leave the country. It is all you need to say, and leave the rest of the talking to me. They shouldn't ask too many questions of a child."

Aniela knew that "they" were the Nazis. She was full of questions, but Papa got up and left the apartment before she could ask them. She rinsed off her breakfast dish, and wondered if she'd ever eat in this kitchen again.

A light snow had begun to fall, so Aniela dressed warmly. Her wool skirt felt itchy, even through her heavy stockings. She began to pack her suitcase. It was hard to decide what to take, with no time to think. Clothes were easy—she did not have many outfits, and only one pair of shoes. She would wear her boots.

What else should she take with her? How could she leave all her beloved old dolls behind? At last, she had to make a difficult choice. Her teddy bear was first to be tucked into the corner of the suitcase. Mama had bought it for her, and she would never part with it. She chose her oldest doll, and the last doll Papa had given her two Christmases ago. Would they celebrate Christmas this year, she wondered? Her favorite music books went into the pocket. She tucked her statue of Mary deep inside her clothes, to keep it from breaking. And last of all, she lay the photograph of her mother on top of everything. She touched her mother's pretty face.

"Where are we going, Mama?" she asked the picture in a whisper.

Papa opened her door. "Ready?"

"Yes, Papa," said Aniela, although she wasn't ready at all. She didn't want to leave Warsaw.

Mr. Kozmyk, the baker, sat in front of the butcher shop in his black sedan. Papa climbed into the front passenger seat, and Aniela into the back. As they drove through the ruined streets of Warsaw, she thought of all her friends and neighbors. What was Edith doing now, she wondered? Was Stefan all right? She knew that Jadzia would cry to find her friend gone, and it made her want to cry, too. But she bit her lip and kept a stony face.

"Are you sure this is the right thing to do, Max?" Mr. Kozmyk asked.

"I have to protect my daughter."

"But you have made a deal with the devil," Mr. Kozmyk said.

Aniela wondered what that meant, but did not dare ask.

"I would sell my soul for her," Papa insisted.

"I hope that your wife's good crystal was enough," Mr. Kozmyk said.

They drove in silence until they reached the train station. Papa shook Mr. Kozmyk's hand. The baker gave Aniela a hug, and slipped something into her pocket. Aniela did not have time to see what it was, for Papa steered her toward the ticket office. There seemed to be Nazi soldiers everywhere. People wrapped in ragged clothes huddled together on benches, and on the floor. No one looked at Aniela as Papa approached the ticket counter. A German officer looked at some papers he had, stamped them, and told them to wait.

"Papa, why did Mr. Kozmyk say that about Mama's crystal?"

"Shh, Aniela," Papa said. "This is no place to talk."

So Aniela sat in silence, huddled close to Papa on the floor because there was no room on the benches. At last, the train pulled into the station. Ragged and weary peasants lined up to board, tickets and papers in hand. German soldiers carefully looked over each paper, then waved the travelers onboard. When they pulled a couple from the line and sent them to stand aside, Aniela felt her heart tighten. Would they also refuse passage to Papa and her?

The German soldier read the paper Papa gave him. He looked up at her father, staring at him for such a long time that Aniela felt afraid. Then he jerked his head toward the door, and Papa pulled Aniela onto the train. He was a little too rough with her, and she cried out. Papa didn't say a word until they were in their seats.

"I'm sorry, Aniela," he said in a low voice. "I was just frightened by that man. I thought my papers would not be good enough for him."

"You're frightened, too, Papa?"

"Only a fool would pretend to be brave these days," Papa said. "Now, why don't you go to sleep?"

"I don't think I can, Papa," Aniela said.

But she rested her head against his arm, and before she knew it she was asleep. When she woke up again, the train was speeding by the rolling, forest-covered hills of the countryside. She stretched and rubbed her eyes.

"Where are we now, Papa?"

"We should be at Thrun soon," Papa said.

Sure enough, the train jerked to a stop just a short while later. Passengers disembarked and new passengers boarded. It took a long time, and Aniela realized she was hungry. She remembered that Mr. Kozmyk had slipped something into her pocket. She reached inside and found a piece of Christmas piernik. The honey cake, made especially for the holidays, was shaped like a snowman.

"Look what Mr. Kozmyk gave us, Papa," she said. "Do you want to share it?"

Papa smiled at her. "No, I'm not hungry. You enjoy it, Aniela."

The piernik was delicious. She wondered how the baker had been able to make it, with so little available to him. How very kind it was for him to give her this little token of Christmas, on a day when Christmas seemed so far away.

Shouts in German filled the air, the doors slammed shut, and the train jerked to a start again. Aniela stared out the window. She saw cattle poking their noses in the snow to find food. The forests were a sparkling fairyland of greens and shimmering white snow. She wondered how long it would take to get to their destination. She turned to ask Papa, but he had fallen asleep.

When a German soldier strode down the aisle, his heavy boots thumping on the wood floor, Aniela closed her own eyes. But the soldier did not believe she was asleep, and spoke as if her eyes were open.

"Where are you going, little fräulein?"

Aniela did not answer, but prayed he would go away.

"Open your eyes," the German insisted. "Don't be rude."

Aniela could not dare disobey him. She didn't want to cause any trouble.

"I'm going to visit my aunt," she said. "She is my mother's sister. She lives in Sweden."

"And how did your Papa manage to get permission to leave the country, little fräulein?"

Aniela did not know the answer to that, so she simply shook her head.

"Of course you wouldn't know, would you?" the German said. "So, what is your aunt's name?"

A flash of panic rose inside Aniela. Papa had never given her make-believe aunt a name. What should she say?

"Well?"

Quickly, Aniela blurted out the first name that came to her mind. It was Papa's sister, who lived in Chicago.

"She is my aunt Elzie," she said.

Now the soldier tapped Papa on the shoulder.

"Wake up," he said.

Papa yawned and blinked his eyes. He gazed up at the soldier.

"You are visiting an aunt in Sweden?"

"Yes, sir," Papa said.

"What is her name?"

Aniela thought she might get sick. Papa would give a different answer, and the German would know they had lied. They would be thrown from the train, perhaps even arrested!

"Her name is Elzie," Papa said. "She is my late wife's sister. She is my daughter's only relative on that side of the family, and she is gravely ill. I thought it was important for Aniela to meet her before she . . . well . . . you know."

The soldier nodded. "All right, then. Go back to sleep, little fräulein."

He said it with a smile, but like most of the soldiers she'd seen, his smile did not reach his eyes. Aniela was glad when he walked away.

Papa leaned close to Aniela and whispered, "I wasn't really asleep."

Aniela grinned at him. He had heard her! It was only a small victory, but it made her feel better.

There were few people at the next station, so it was a quick stop. But shortly after the train rolled away again, it came to a screeching halt. The scream of the brakes made Aniela cringe. She had to grab Papa's arm so she wouldn't be thrown from her seat. Everyone around her began to talk, and someone in the back of the car moaned that he was bleeding. There was a woman with a baby across the aisle. The jolting stop had startled the infant awake, and he wailed loudly as his mother tried to comfort him.

Aniela looked out the window. There was nothing to see but a vast white blanket of snow, and a forest of bare trees.

"Papa, why have we stopped here?" she asked. "There is no station."

"I don't know, Aniela," Papa said.

A soldier strode through the car, ignoring the questions and cries for help around him. He pushed on into the next car, the door slamming behind him. Aniela watched through her window, and saw a family being dragged from the train. There was a mother and father, a little boy, and a girl of about her own age. She could not hear their words through the glass, but she could tell the man was pleading with the Nazi officer who waved a gun at him.

Aniela *did* hear the quick shot of a pistol, though. The man fell to the ground as his wife and children screamed in terror.

"Oh, Papa!" she cried. "They killed that man!"

"Shh," Papa said. "Turn away from there. Don't look!"

Aniela obeyed him, and buried her face in his sleeve. But she thought she would never forget the picture of that man slumping to the ground, as his family watched in horror.

"Just one of many," she heard the man across the aisle say.

"Monsters," said a woman.

"You'd better stop talking," said a third person. "Or you might end up like him."

With a great jolt, the train started to roll again. Aniela pulled away from her father and looked out the window. The woman and her children knelt by the father's body, their suitcases broken open and their belongings scattered around them.

"Papa, how can they leave them like that?"

"How can they do anything they do?" Papa asked. "Say no more about it, Aniela."

It almost seemed that Papa didn't care. But Aniela knew he was only pretending because no one in that train car dared speak up against the Nazis. How easy would it be for each one of them to fall victim to a Nazi bullet? Aniela closed her eyes and prayed for the dead man and his family, even though she did not know who they were.

Chapter Nine

ANIELA knew she would never forget this train ride. Each time the big locomotive stopped, she was terrified that she and Papa would be dragged off and left in the middle of a snowy nowhere, just like that other unfortunate family. Surely, someone would discover their lie, and know that they weren't going to visit a sick aunt in Sweden.

But, at last, the train reached Koszalin. It was late in the day, and Papa found them a room in a small inn near the docks. They shared a meal of kielbasa and sauerkraut, but they were both so tired they hardly spoke to each other: Then they went straight to bed. The next morning, they joined a line of others waiting to board a ferry to Sweden. Signs of war surrounded them, from the tumbled-down remains of old buildings to the line of Nazi jeeps parked along the street. Swastikas, those broken crosses that Aniela hated so much, seemed to be everywhere.

Aniela clung to Papa's coat sleeve, and watched as cars were driven onto the ferry. Then the people were directed onboard. Once again, Papa had to take out his papers. Aniela held her breath, afraid they would be turned back this time, but they were allowed passage. Papa found them a seat on a hard wooden bench. At last, the ferry pulled away from the dock.

Aniela thought she might cry. She watched as the boat pulled away from the coast of her country, and felt as if something pulled at her own heart, as well.

"Papa, may I stand at the railing?"

"Let's go together, Aniela," Papa said, in a sad, quiet voice. He stood up and took her hand.

Aniela tried to ignore the Nazi soldiers who stood nearby with rifles slung across their backs. After a while, she could no longer see Poland. With a sigh, she turned away from the railing.

"Papa, I'm hungry," she said.

Papa took her to a booth where they could buy some food. Aniela wanted to ask Papa what they would do when they reached Sweden, but she didn't dare. Not with soldiers standing so close. She was glad when the ferry reached the new land, and they were allowed to enter the country. Before his arrest, Stefan had explained to her that Sweden was a neutral country, which meant they did not take sides with anyone. When she saw that the Nazi soldiers did not disembark, she began to relax for the first time that day. Papa led her from the ship and away from the docks.

"What are we going to do now, Papa?" Aniela asked as they walked down a narrow cobblestone street.

"We'll find ourselves a place to stay," Papa said. "And I will send a telegram on to your aunt Elzie and uncle Stanislaus."

"You'll let them know we are safe?"

"Yes, Aniela. But there's more. I could not speak of it before without danger. Aniela, we are going to America."

Aniela stopped and put her suitcase down.

"Papa!"

"I know it is a surprise," Papa said. He picked up Aniela's bag himself. "Come, it's late and we need to find a room."

He walked away, and Aniela hurried after him.

"Papa, you never told me we would go to America!"

"I did not know it myself," Papa replied. "You can't simply buy passage on a ship, you know. It took a lot of work to get us this far. Stefan helped me get the papers I needed to leave the country."

Aniela grieved to think of her piano teacher. She was free now, but he wasn't. It didn't seem fair.

"Did they arrest Stefan because he helped us?"

"Because he helped a lot of people," Papa said. "May God watch over him."

Papa tilted his head up, and Aniela saw a sign hanging from the side of a brick building. It was written in Swedish, with an English translation below: THE VIK-

ING INN. It made her think of the sign outside Jadzia's door. By now, Jadzia probably wondered what had happened to her friend. Aniela was sad when she thought of her two best friends, Jadzia and Edith, for she was pretty certain she would never see either of them again.

"We'll stay here," Papa said. "And tomorrow morning, I'll send that telegram. Your aunt will help us get to America."

A week went by without an answer from America. Even though Sweden was a beautiful country, and Papa insisted they were safe, Aniela was afraid to leave her hotel room. She had heard Papa talk of spies, and wondered if there could be people like that here, too—people who would love to send them back to their homeland, to face horrible punishment for tricking the Nazis.

Aniela did not pay much attention to the dates on the calendar. She watched through her window as shoppers hurried down the streets laden with Christmas presents. Carols played on the radio, and the hotel lobby was decorated beautifully. But Aniela didn't care. What kind of Christmas could she have, thinking how the Nazis might be hurting Stefan? And she'd never celebrated the holiday without Jadzia. Thoughts of the wonderful food Jadzia's mother always made on Christmas, when she would invite Aniela and Papa to dinner, made Aniela want to weep.

Before she knew it, Christmas Eve had arrived.

Papa insisted they should attend Midnight Mass. They had not been to church since the Nazis occupied Warsaw and closed up St. Hedwig's. Aniela put on her good dress and tied a ribbon in her hair. She wanted to look properly dressed, and yet inside her heart she did not see why they were doing this.

"I know you feel sad, Aniela," Papa said as he combed his hair, "but we must not ever forget that it is Christ's birthday we celebrate. We must not let evil take that away from us."

"Yes, Papa," Aniela said.

She clung to his hand as they walked to the nearest church. Friendly faces turned to them when they entered, but Aniela still kept close to her father. She did not understand a word of the Swedish service, but followed the examples of the others and knew when to kneel or stand. It was interesting to hear familiar carols such as "Oh, Little Town of Bethlehem" sung in a foreign tongue. The manger scene on the altar was beautiful, and dozens of candles cast a warm glow on everyone. When they were walking home again, she asked Papa about Christmas Day.

"We can't really celebrate this year, can we?" she asked.

"You never know what will happen," Papa said.

They reached the hotel. Papa ordered Aniela directly to bed, for it was very late. She fell asleep almost immediately. The next thing she knew, someone was singing "Away in a Manger" on the radio, in English.

She opened her eyes to see it was morning. Christmas morning.

Last year, and all the years before that, she had jumped out of bed to run and see what presents awaited her. There was always a lovely new dress, new sheet music for the piano, and many other treats. But she knew there would be nothing this year. Papa had risked his life to save her from the Nazis, and that was enough of a gift.

But when she went into the little parlor that connected to their bedroom, she saw one of her stockings pinned to the curtain. She rushed to it and pulled it down. To her delight, she found a shiny red apple, some walnuts, and chocolate candies!

"I know it isn't a new book or dress," Papa said, as he came from the bathroom, "and we don't have a fireplace here, either. But I hope it brings you a little Christmas cheer, Aniela."

"Oh, Papa!" Aniela cried. She ran to hug him. "It's the most wonderful gift! An apple, Papa! A real apple! And chocolate! Thank you so much! Thank you!"

Papa laughed. "You enjoy it all, little one. And next year, I will give you the Christmas you deserve."

Aniela had not had an apple, or any other piece of good fruit, in months. How she savored it! It was crispy and juicy, and when she was done there was not a bit of it left but the smallest core and stem. She saved the walnuts and candies, and ate them one at a time over the next days. Each time she did so, she thought that she had the kindest, most wonderful father in all the world.

Aniela was very happy when two tickets on a steamship to New York City arrived shortly after the New Year. Up to now, she had hardly believed they really were going to America. She thought someone would stop them and send them back to Warsaw. But it was as if a guardian angel watched over them.

Aniela remembered the strange words Mr. Kozmyk had spoken just before he left them at the Warsaw train depot. What had he meant about Papa making a deal with the devil? She had tried to ask Papa about that, but he'd refused to answer.

"You only need to know that you are safe with me," Papa said. "It doesn't matter to a young girl how adults do things, does it?"

"No, Papa," Aniela had said, but she thought it really did matter. Still, children were never supposed to question adults. Papa didn't want to talk about it, and so Aniela had to respect him and stop her questions.

They took a bus to the port in Göteborg. When they boarded the ship to America, Papa showed his papers as before. But this time, the woman who looked at them had a warm, friendly face. She smiled at Aniela, and spoke to her with a Swedish accent that Aniela found very musical.

"I hope you enjoy your visit to America," she said. "It's a beautiful country."

"Papa tells me that, too," Aniela said.

Their berth was a little room with white walls and

no windows, down in the lower part of the ship called "steerage." The bunks were small, and there was hardly enough room for their suitcases. But it was clean and comfortable, and it meant something important to Aniela: It meant they were on their way to happiness and freedom. Maybe the Nazis had taken that away from them in Poland, but they would not dare try such a thing with a big, strong country like America!

During their passage, Aniela made a few friends on board. They played games on the deck and sometimes sat together for meals. One girl was an American from Ohio, who told the others all about her country. The more she spoke, the more excited Aniela became about her new home.

One day, as Aniela explored the ship, she found a woman playing piano in the empty dining hall. Aniela and Papa were too poor to eat here, but Aniela often sat outside and listened to the band. The doorway was open, and she stood there as the woman played. She spotted Aniela and smiled. She was a beautiful lady, with long blond hair and blue eyes.

"Hello, dear," she said. "Why don't you come inside?"

Aniela hesitated. After all, she was only a steerage passenger.

"Is it all right?" she asked.

"Of course," said the woman. "My name is Liddy. I've seen you outside the dining hall before, haven't I?"

"Yes," Aniela said, and felt a little embarrassed. "I . . . I like the music."

"What's your name, dear?"

"Aniela," Aniela said, and came to stand closer. The woman smelled of flowery perfume. It was so much nicer than the death and fire Aniela had breathed for so long.

"My mama played piano," Aniela told her. "And someday, I will, too!"

"Do you play at all now?" Liddy asked.

"Oh, yes," Aniela said. "But I had to stop when the Nazis took my piano teacher away—and then my piano, too! They take everything!"

Liddy looked very sad now. Aniela knew Liddy felt sorry for her. The woman moved aside and patted the piano bench.

"Would you like to play a little?" she asked.

"Oh, yes, thank you!" Aniela said with a smile.

She played some of her favorite Christmas carols. A small crowd gathered, and when she was done, they applauded her. Blushing, Aniela thanked Liddy and ran to tell her father what had happened. She found him on the foredeck, playing gin rummy with a friend.

When Aniela finished her story, Papa smiled proudly.

"I'm sure you played beautifully," he said.

Papa traded one of his cards for a card on the table. Then he smiled at the skinny man with a mustache who sat across from him. He set his cards down.

"Gin!"

"You are too good at this game, Max Kaminski," the man said.

Aniela tapped Papa's shoulder.

"Papa, when we get to America, can I take lessons again?" she asked.

Papa sighed. "I don't know, little one. It might be hard for us for a while, but we'll try our best, won't we?"

Aniela nodded, and watched as Papa dealt another hand. She wondered why it seemed that every day that went by there were more and more questions without answers. Why would America be hard for them? Wouldn't Aunt Elzie and Uncle Stanislaus take care of them? And wasn't America a wonderful place where everyone was rich and no one was afraid?

IT was an icy cold day when the ship finally reached the shores of America. Everyone on board, from the richest passenger to the poorest, stood on deck and watched as the Statue of Liberty came into view.

"She is beautiful, isn't she?" Papa said.

"I wish we had a real lady like her in Warsaw," Aniela replied. "The Nazis could never fight her!"

"And she will keep us safe here, too," Papa promised.

It took several hours for all the immigrants to be processed at Ellis Island. Papa exchanged his Polish currency for American money. Then they boarded a ferry to Manhattan Island. After they embarked, Papa took a letter from his pocket, read it silently, and led Aniela to a police officer. Aniela stiffened, for she could not help thinking of the Nazi officers back in Warsaw.

Papa showed the letter to the man. As soon as Aniela saw his warm smile, she knew he was a friend.

"You need to get to Pennsylvania Station," the policeman said. "Ask for a train to Chicago. It's easy enough. Do you want me to get a taxi for you, sir?"

"No, we can walk," Papa said. "Thank you for your help."

The policeman jotted down directions on a piece of paper. Papa and Aniela walked for blocks in search of the train station. Aniela couldn't stop staring at the tall buildings around her. The streets were so crowded she kept bumping into people. When she saw the Empire State Building, she grabbed hold of her father.

"Papa, it won't fall down, will it?"

Papa laughed. "It's very strong, Aniela."

Pennsylvania Station was just a short distance away. Papa spoke to a woman behind a ticket counter, and purchased two train tickets.

"The train does not leave until early tomorrow morning," Papa said. "We will have to sleep on one of the benches here."

He found a locker and put their luggage inside. Then he took Aniela back up to the street again. Snow flurries blew everywhere, and the smell coming from a vendor's cart of pretzels and chestnuts made Aniela very hungry.

"Can we get some dinner, Papa?"

"Yes, I'd like that," said Papa.

He looked around, and spotted a kindly looking older couple.

"Please, do you know a good place to eat?" he asked, his Polish accent thick.

The couple frowned at each other, unable to understand him. The man called over another man, who wore a uniform that was different from the police officer who had helped them on the docks. Aniela saw the train pin on his lapel and knew he was a conductor. He listened to Papa, then pointed to a building nearby. A few minutes later, they entered a restaurant called an "automat." Aniela thought it was the funniest restaurant she had ever seen. You put a quarter into a slot and a little door opened to give you a sandwich.

"America is full of so many wonders, Papa!" she cried.

Papa nodded. "It isn't our Poland, but it is a great country. We will like it here, won't we?"

"I think we will, Papa," Aniela agreed.

Chapter Ten

EARLY the next morning, Aniela and Papa once again boarded a train for a long ride. Papa bought a movie magazine for Aniela to read. She enjoyed the pictures of all the wonderful Hollywood stars. Aniela was glad that her English was adequate, because it was fun to read the articles, too. She liked the one about Clark Gable the best. It helped make the time go by faster.

When she grew tired of reading, Aniela looked out the window. The passing countryside, dotted with farms and forests and little towns, made her think of Poland. Perhaps, in some ways America wasn't so different from her homeland. She felt a little homesick, but told herself that this would be a great new adventure. She would write to Jadzia as soon as she could, and tell her about all the remarkable new things she had seen.

Papa bought them mugs of soup and little packages of crackers from the dining car. It was too expensive to sit at the tables there, so they brought their food back to their seats. He told Aniela some stories he remembered of the trip he and Mama had made to America long ago. Aniela decided she couldn't wait to see these places for herself.

Soon, tired from the long trip, Aniela fell asleep. The jerk of the train, as it came to a halt, woke her later. All around her, people stood up and gathered their belongings.

"Are we here, Papa?" she asked.

"Yes, we've reached Chicago," Papa said. "Come now, Aniela. Your uncle Stanislaus should be waiting for us."

A cheerful woman's voice called out Papa's name as soon as they got off the train. When Aniela saw the family hurrying toward them, she almost dropped her suitcase. Aunt Elzie looked so much like Mama! Of course, she was older than Mama was in Aniela's photograph, and a little plumper. But Aunt Elzie had the same dark, almond eyes and brown curls as both Mama and Aniela herself.

"Oh, look at you!" Aunt Elzie cried. She took Aniela's face in her hands. "What a beautiful young lady!"

She pulled Aniela close and gave her a warm hug. Then, with her arms still around Aniela, she turned to Papa.

"Max, she's so thin," Aunt Elzie said.

"We don't have much food in Poland," Papa replied with a frown.

Now Uncle Stanislaus pushed forward and offered Papa his hand to shake.

"Well, we've sure got plenty here!" he cried. "Welcome to America, Max!"

He was tall and lanky. There were lines etched down his face, and his mustache tickled Aniela's cheek when he kissed her. He had the biggest smile Aniela had ever seen, and she liked him at once. He patted her head.

"Hello, Aniela," he said. "You call me Uncle Stan, okay? Well, you certainly do look like your mother."

"Yes, she's the image of Helena," Aunt Elzie agreed.

There were two boys that Aniela guessed were her cousins. The smaller boy began to giggle.

"Say hello to your uncle Max and cousin Aniela, boys," Uncle Stan said. "Max, Aniela, this is Henryk and Leopold."

"Hi," the boys said in unison.

Henryk was tall and thin like his father, with the same sandy-colored hair and blue eyes. Leopold's dark curls surrounded a cherubic face that was spattered with freckles.

"Henryk is fourteen," Aunt Elzie said, "and Leopold is seven."

Leopold tugged at his father's coat sleeve.

"Daddy, call me Leo," he said.

"Yes, yes, your American name," Uncle Stan said. "And Henryk likes to be called Hank."

Uncle Stan took Aniela's bag and led the family away from the platform.

"Do you want an American name, too, Aniela?" asked Hank.

"I don't know," Aniela replied hesitantly.

"Well, we'll give you one anyway," Hank insisted. "Nellie. Your new American name is Nellie."

Aniela thought about this for a moment, then she smiled. "Nellie. I like that! It's very pretty!"

"Ooooh, it's so pretty," Leo said in a mocking tone, as he made a silly face.

Hank cuffed him across the ear, but so gently Leo only laughed at him. Everyone piled into Uncle Stan's car. How big and comfortable it was, Aniela thought. No one she knew had a car like this in Warsaw!

It was a short drive to Uncle Stan and Aunt Elzie's house. Along the way, the adults talked about the troubles in Europe. Aniela looked out the window; unable to get enough of all the new sights. Leo and Hank teased each other constantly, but she hardly heard them. She kept thinking of her new name. Nellie, Nellie, Nellie. What would Jadzia and Edith think of that?

Uncle Stan pulled into the gravel-covered driveway of a large white house. It had a bright blue front door and blue shutters at the windows. The remains of a recent snowfall dotted the lawn, and bare rosebushes awaited the coming spring.

The train ride had taken the entire day. Aniela did

not realize how terribly hungry she was until she walked into the house and smelled something cooking. Papa breathed in deeply as he took off his coat.

"It's a turkey!" Leo told them. "A turkey and stuffing and mashed potatoes and . . ."

Suddenly, Aniela burst into tears. She simply could not help herself. She had heard stories of America, but she had never imagined they could be true. A real dinner waited for them, not just soup boiled from oxtails and turnips! Was this only a wonderful dream? Would she wake up at any moment and find that she had to go down to Nazi headquarters and play for Commander Himmel and his horrid officers? Was it only make-believe that Papa had saved her?

"Oh, Aniela!" Aunt Elzie said. Once again, she took the girl into her arms.

"How come she's crying like that?" Leo asked.

"She's just overwhelmed," said Uncle Stan. "Elzie, why don't you take her in to her room? Boys, we have a meal to put on the table."

"That's girls' work!" Hank protested.

"Henryk!" his father snapped in a warning tone.

Moaning, the boys followed him into the kitchen. Max joined them. Aunt Elzie took Aniela into her room. It was about the same size as the one she'd left in Warsaw. There was no window seat, but she could see a big oak tree with a swing in the backyard. There was a brass bed with a white chenille spread, a small white dresser, and some empty shelves.

"You can put your things out as you like," Aunt

Elzie said. "But why don't you rest first? You've been through so much!"

Aniela felt better now. She even felt a little silly for crying like that.

"I'd like to unpack my things, Aunt Elzie," she said. "And I'm very hungry."

"Of course you are," Aunt Elzie said. "Why, I'd wager you haven't had a good square meal in months! You just get yourself settled in, and as soon as you and your father are ready, we'll eat."

Aniela set her suitcase on the bed and opened it. She unpacked everything. She put her clothes in the dresser and lined up her dolls and music books on the shelves. The old teddy bear took a place of honor at the head of the brass bed. Mama's picture went on the nightstand. Aniela kissed the photo.

"I think I'm going to like America, Mama," she said. "Aunt Elzie looks so much like you!"

She changed from her heavy snow boots, wool skirt, and sweater into a dark blue jumper with a white blouse. Then she went into the dining room. The family sat down for a wonderful meal, one Aniela knew she would never forget. Everything was so delicious! She had three helpings of turkey.

"Boy, you sure do eat a lot," Leo remarked.

"Leo Kubek, you mind your manners," Aunt Elzie scolded.

"You're welcome to as much as you want, Aniela," Uncle Stan said.

Papa took another roll from the basket in front of him.

"You have been so kind to us," he said. "I keep thinking it will all go away soon."

Aniela was surprised to hear that Papa also feared this was just a dream.

"It's here to stay," Uncle Stan said. "We've had our tough times in America, but things are changing. And you're welcome to share with us as long as you need to."

"Hitler certainly changed things in Europe," Papa said. His face was dark and grim. "Life will never be the same for the people of Poland."

"Well, he'll certainly never hurt us!" Aunt Elzie insisted. "We're a big ocean away from all that trouble!"

Papa buttered his roll. It looked so good to Aniela that she took another one for herself, too. Real butter tasted so wonderful.

"Do you think the Americans will join the war?" Papa asked.

"I hope not," Uncle Stan said. "I think it's best we leave it up to the French and British to fight Adolf Hitler and his minions."

"Oh, Pops," Hank moaned. "Do we hafta talk about dumb stuff like war?"

"I want a gun!" Leo cried. He held his fork like a gun and began to shoot everyone at the table. "Just like Dick Tracy! Bang! Bang!"

Aniela bowed her head. She couldn't help thinking of the real guns she'd seen, real guns that had taken innocent lives.

"Stop it, Leo," Uncle Stan ordered. He seemed to understand Aniela's distress.

When the meal was finished, Aniela went into the kitchen to help Aunt Elzie with the dishes.

"Do you remember my mama?" she asked.

"Oh, yes," Aunt Elzie said. "What a beautiful, talented woman! How sad it was that her heart was not strong. She would have been world famous by now, I'm sure."

"My piano teacher said she might have been as well known as Ignacy Jan Paderewski," Aniela said.

"I believe that," Aunt Elzie said. "And she had such a good spirit that everyone would have loved her."

She handed Aniela a plate to dry. "I hear that you play piano, too?"

"Yes, Aunt Elzie," Aniela said. "But one day the Nazis came and arrested my piano teacher. And then they came and took away everything in his apartment, even the piano!"

She put the dish on the pile she had dried already. "Do you have a piano?" she asked.

"I'm sorry, but we don't," Aunt Elzie said. "We would buy you one if we could, but times have been hard and we can't afford it."

Aniela thought of the remarkable meal she'd just finished, of the big, comfortable car her uncle drove, and of this pretty house. Then she thought how hard life had been in Warsaw since the bombings. How could Aunt Elzie say times had been hard here?

Aunt Elzie seemed to read her mind.

"I know everything here looks grand, and I'm sure it is, compared to what you've lived with these past months. But America has been in a terrible way for a long time. Many people have been without jobs and homes. We've called this time 'The Great Depression.' Your uncle Stan says times are changing, but few people are secure yet."

"Then you are really poor?" Aniela asked.

Aunt Elzie laughed. "Oh, no! Not at all! We have plenty to share with you and your papa, and you will always be welcome here. This is your new home, Aniela!"

Aniela smiled at her aunt. They finished cleaning the kitchen, singing Polish folk songs as they did so. Aunt Elzie had barely put away the last dish when Leo burst into the room.

"Hurry up, Mommy!" he cried. "It's time for *Amos 'n' Andy!*"

Aniela and Papa joined their relatives as they gathered around a big radio in the living room. Aniela was amazed at the show she heard. Radio Poland had been silent for so long that she'd almost forgotten what it was like to hear a voice from far away. She didn't understand some of the things the two characters in the show said, but it was fun to see Papa laughing. It had been too long since he'd laughed out loud.

They listened to several more shows, and shared wonderful angel food cake for dessert. Later, Uncle Stan read a magazine, Aunt Elzie crocheted, and Hank read the comics to Leo as music played in the background. Papa rested in a big, comfortable chair with his eyes closed, but Aniela knew he was awake because he tapped his fingers in time to the orchestra music.

"Time for bed, Leo," Aunt Elzie announced at eight-thirty.

"I'm not tired," Leo insisted, and then yawned loudly. He protested all the way to his room, but soon was quiet. Aniela felt tired herself, so she was glad when Aunt Elzie told Hank and her to go to bed at nine.

"We have to get up for church in the morning," Aunt Elzie said.

Aniela found a pile of neatly folded towels on her bed. Aunt Elzie drew her a bath with piles and piles of bubbles, then left her alone. Aniela pretended she was a movie star. She blew at the bubbles the way she'd seen Rita Hayworth do in one movie. She styled her shampoo-covered hair into fancy shapes. It had seemed a lifetime had gone by since she'd last felt like playing. It was so wonderful that a long time passed before someone knocked at the door.

"Did you fall asleep in there?" Aunt Elzie asked.

"No, Aunt Elzie!" Aniela said. "I'm coming out now!"

Her bed was so comfortable, and she felt so safe, that Aniela slept soundly all night long. The next morning, she put on her best dress for church and joined her family as they walked to St. Stanislaus Cathedral. Another family walked in front of them. There were two parents, an older boy, and a girl about Aniela's age. The girl kept turning and staring back over her shoulder.

"Good morning, Gloria, good morning, Frank," Uncle Stan greeted. "Come meet my brother-in-law and his daughter."

Uncle Stan introduced everyone as they walked. Aniela learned the boy was named Carl and the girl was Judy. Judy hooked an arm through Aniela's and pulled her away from the others.

"Sit with me at Mass," she said.

"All right," Aniela agreed.

Aniela was delighted that the Mass was said in her native Polish. Later, Aunt Elzie explained that most services were said in Latin, but one Mass each Sunday was offered in Polish.

"It is a good way for the children to remember our language," she said.

"Can Aniela have breakfast at my house, Mrs. Kubek?" Judy asked.

"Of course she can," Aunt Elzie said. "You girls have fun getting to know each other."

Judy and her family lived just a few houses away from Aunt Elzie and Uncle Stan. Her mother made pancakes for everyone. Once again, Aniela thought she was in heaven.

"Oh, real syrup!" she cried. "And real butter! We don't have butter at all, and the only syrup I have had in a long time was when my friend Jadzia's mother made some from beet roots."

"Beet root syrup," Carl said. "Sounds awful."

"Not everyone is as blessed as we are, Carl," said his mother. She smiled at Aniela. "You enjoy it as much as you want!"

Judy poured a glass of juice for her. Aniela did not remember the last time she tasted orange juice.

"You had a friend named Jadzia?" Judy asked. "That's funny. My name in Polish is 'Jadzia.' "

"Really?" Aniela said, amazed.

How funny that she should meet a new friend in America with the same name as her friend back home!

"And my American name is Nellie," Aniela said. "Can you call me Nellie from now on?"

"You bet," Judy agreed. "We're gonna be great friends. I'm so happy there's finally someone my own age in this neighborhood!"

"And I'm so happy to have made a new friend so fast," Aniela said.

The two girls smiled at each other. Judy was slender, with dark eyes and straight, chestnut-colored hair she wore pulled back with a headband. She had on a pretty red dress with long puffy sleeves and a white collar. Aniela thought her own dress was dark and dreary. But she would not complain about it. She would never complain about anything, ever again. Not when she had been given so very much in such a short time—a fine new home, delicious food, and, best of all, a new friend!

Chapter Eleven

AFTER dinner that night, Aniela sat down and wrote a letter to Jadzia. She told her about the train ride, and how frightened she had been that they might be caught and sent to jail. She told about the ferry ride, Christmas in the little hotel room in Sweden, and about the ship's voyage across the Atlantic Ocean. She imagined how impressed Jadzia would be to hear that Aniela saw the real Statue of Liberty. They'd only seen a picture of it in their history books—before the history books had been taken away by the Nazis.

I don't care if I ever board another train in my whole life, Jadzia! At least the American train ride did not scare me. And Papa bought me a movie magazine that was fun to read. Maybe I will meet the real Clark Gable!

I miss you so much, my dear friend. I wish we did not have to sneak away like we did. I wish you could come to America and meet the girl with your name, my new friend, Judy. That is your name in American. And I'm called "Nellie" here. Isn't that funny? I have been here little more than a day, but already I feel like an American. Now, I only wish I could start my piano lessons again. I think about Stefan a lot, and pray that he is safe. Edith, too. And you! I will never, ever, ever forget you!

Aniela wrote her name with a flourish, adding a little heart at the end. Judy signed her name like that, and she thought it was very pretty. She put the letter into an envelope, wrote down Jadzia's address, and carried it into the living room. Papa was reading the newspaper, Uncle Stan and Leo worked on a jigsaw puzzle, and Aunt Elzie crocheted an afghan. Hank was busy with a model ship he was building. Music played softly on the radio.

"Aunt Elzie?" Aniela said.

Aunt Elzie looked up as she crocheted the moss green yarn.

"Yes, dear?"

"I have a letter I'd like to mail," Aniela said. "It's for my best friend, back in Poland."

She heard Papa's newspaper rustle and turned to

see he had put it down. Uncle Stan looked over from the puzzle, first at his wife, and then at Papa. All the adults looked very worried.

"Aniela, I'm afraid you can't do that," Papa said finally.

"Why?"

"It is simply too dangerous," Papa said.

Uncle Stan stood up and came to sit on the couch next to Aunt Elzie. He leaned forward, resting his thin arms on his knees and folding his hands.

"Max, you really should explain things to her," he said.

"She doesn't need to know anything," Papa insisted. "She's a child."

"She'll be thirteen very soon!" Aunt Elzie said. "You've taken her from the only home she's ever known, into a strange place . . ."

Aniela stepped forward, her hand held out.

"Oh, but I like it here!" she said.

Aunt Elzie smiled up at her. "I know you do, dear. But your papa is right. You can't have any contact with your friends in Poland. At least, not until the war is over."

Hank snorted, and turned to them with a tube of glue in his hand.

"Some war," he said. "There hasn't been any fighting in months. They all seem to be standing around doing nothing over there. My teacher says people call it the 'Phony War.' "

"And let us pray to God it stays that way," Uncle Stan said.

"Let us pray to God someone shoots that monster," Papa growled.

"Daddy, what's a phony war?" Leo asked.

"It means that the British and French are waiting for the Germans to make the next move," his father said. "No one is fighting right now."

Aniela crouched down on the floor next to Papa's chair.

"Papa, I'm a big girl now," she said. "Please tell me what is happening. Does it have something to do with what Mr. Kozmyk said? About you making a deal with the devil?"

Papa sighed. "Yes, Aniela. You see, I knew there could only be trouble if you were ever to set foot in Commander Himmel's house. The things the Nazis might do to a young girl . . ."

"Max," Aunt Elzie said, her tone warning him to go no further.

Papa waved a hand at her.

"I had to act quickly," Papa said. "It was a desperate time that called for desperate measures. I sold the butcher shop, and all of your mother's fine china and crystal."

"Oh, no, Papa!" Aniela said. She had thought perhaps that one day they might go back for it all.

"I used the money to get the paperwork I needed for us to leave," Papa said. "And the man who arranged this for me was Commander Himmel himself."

Aniela frowned, confused. "Commander Himmel helped us escape?"

"Yeah, a Nazi helped you escape," Hank sneered.

"Hank, go to your room," Uncle Stan ordered.

"Pops!"

"March!"

Aniela cringed a little. It always scared her when someone, who was usually nice, became stern and angry. With a growl, Hank put down the mast he'd been gluing and left the room. Uncle Stan looked at Leo, and tilted his head toward the hallway. He didn't want the little boy to hear this. Leo obeyed at once, and earned a smile of approval from his father.

"I don't understand, Papa," Aniela said.

"The Germans are very poor people, Aniela," Papa said. "Money talks to them. At least, it spoke to Commander Himmel. He did not do this through the goodness of his heart—if there can be any goodness in a blackened heart—but through pure greed. It was his signature that got us to Sweden. But we weren't supposed to get farther than that. Do you remember how I took my money out of the bank a long time ago?"

"Yes, Papa."

"I sensed we would need it someday," Papa said. "And I was right. It took almost every *zloty* I had to pay for this trip. But it was all worth it, to see you safe and secure here."

Aniela thought about this for a long time. Papa had dared to ask Commander Himmel for help? And the Nazi had given it to him? Yes, it was like making a deal with the devil. But what had Papa said? It was desperate times that called for desperate measures. And how more desperate could you be than when an enemy had taken over your life?

She stood up and leaned forward to embrace her father tightly around the neck.

"You risked your life to save me," she said. "That is not a deal with the devil, Papa. It is the work of a saint."

"Amen to that!" Aunt Elzie agreed.

"I love you, Papa," said Aniela.

"And I love you, little one," Papa said. "But do you understand now why you can't mail that letter?"

Sadly, Aniela looked down at the pink envelope.

"Will I ever see Jadzia again?" she asked. "Will I ever see Edith, or Stefan?"

"Perhaps, someday," Papa said.

Aunt Elzie put her afghan aside and stood up.

"I have some nice chocolate ice cream in the freezer," she said. "Let's all have dessert?"

Aniela knew that Aunt Elzie wanted to make her feel better. She followed her into the kitchen, where she helped dish out bowls of chocolate ice cream, peanuts, and chocolate sauce. Aunt Elzie told her it was called a tin roof sundae. Uncle Stan even let the boys out to have some. Aniela thought about her friends back in Poland as she ate it, and hoped that at this very moment they also enjoyed some little bit of happiness.

WHEN Hank and Leo left for school the next morning, their mother stood on the porch and watched them walk to the corner. Aniela stood at her side. Both boys turned to wave, and then turned in opposite directions.

"We live very close to all the schools in the area," Aunt Elzie said. "You won't need to ride the school bus."

"When can I go to school, Aunt Elzie?" Aniela asked.

"In a few days," Aunt Elzie said. "I've already spoken to them about you, and you are registered. But you'll need some new clothes and supplies."

Aniela looked down at her brown coat and brown shoes.

"Could it be something with lots of color, Aunt Elzie?"

Aunt Elzie laughed. "Of course! In fact, Judy has offered to come with us after school today to help you choose some new things."

Aniela couldn't wait for her friend to come home. Many times during the next hours, she walked out on the porch and gazed down the street. When she finally saw Judy turn the corner, she waved excitedly. Judy hurried up to her.

"This is going to be so much fun!" Judy cried.

"I will be happy to see the new American fashions," Aniela said.

They had to wait for Leo and Hank to come home. Aunt Elzie left Hank to babysit, with orders not to have friends in the house. Hank wasn't happy about this, and he gave Aniela a dirty look. She paid no attention to him. She was too happy to let him worry her.

They went to Campus Girl Fashions, a downtown boutique. Judy helped Aniela pick things out, and soon she entered the dressing room with her favorites. When she came out, she wore a pink sweater set, a knee-length beige skirt that stopped just above her knees, little white sox and saddle shoes. Aunt Elzie clapped her hands once and smiled with approval.

"You look wonderful!" she said. "Judy made some good choices for you."

Aniela looked down at her black-and-white shoes.

"Saddle shoes," she said. "How funny! It sounds like something a horse would wear."

Judy laughed. "The black part looks like saddles, Nellie. Now . . ."

She reached toward Aniela's hair and played with it a moment. Then she turned to Aunt Elzie.

"Can we take her to the beauty parlor today?" she asked. "She'd look cute with one of the new hairdos."

"Oh, can I, Aunt Elzie?" Aniela asked hopefully. "Then I'll look like a real American girl!"

"Of course," Aunt Elzie said.

She paid for the clothes Judy had helped Aniela choose. They placed the bags in the trunk of the car, then walked down the street to the beauty parlor. Aniela sniffed at the strange smells in the air. She had never been to a beauty parlor, but had only sat in a barbershop when Papa had his hair cut. Sometimes, Mr. Frank, the barber, had given her curls a little trim.

"What can I do for you?" asked a pretty woman with silvery hair.

"I want a new American hairstyle," Aniela said in her thick Polish accent.

"My niece is newly arrived from Poland, Martha," Aunt Elzie said. She knew the beautician well.

Martha gave Aniela a sympathetic smile. It was a smile she saw a lot, whenever anyone heard where she was from. Aniela guessed that most everyone had heard of the hard times her people were facing now.

"You just sit right down, dear," Martha said.

She wrapped a plastic shawl around Aniela's shoulders, then began to play with her curls as she looked at Aniela's reflection in the mirror.

"My, what beautiful thick hair you have," she said.

Then she went to work. When she was finished, most of Aniela's curls lay on the floor. Her pretty face was now surrounded by soft waves. Martha parted her hair on the side and pulled the longer half back with a ribbon. Aniela turned to Judy and Aunt Elzie, touching her new hairstyle.

"Do you like it? It is pretty?"

"You look terrific, Nellie," Judy said.

"You're very beautiful, Aniela," Aunt Elzie agreed.

A few days later, dressed in her new clothes, her hair tied back in a pretty ribbon, Aniela felt very confident as she walked to her first day of American school. But when she saw the huge double doors of the Green

Street Middle School, she stopped in her tracks as if frozen to the sidewalk. Judy pulled her a little.

"Come on," she said. "We'll be late!"

"Oh, Judy!" Aniela cried. "I'm scared! I thought it would be easy—but this isn't my Polish school! I don't know anyone here, and they speak only English, and they'll have different rules and . . ."

Judy rolled her eyes. "It's just a school, Nellie. Our teacher, Mrs. Smith, is very nice. And if you don't understand something in English, I can explain it in Polish."

She started to walk, and Aniela followed her.

"Besides," Judy said, "you speak better English than some of the kids here, and they were born in America!"

Aniela was still nervous when Judy pushed the doors open and they walked into the long, locker-lined hallway. A moment later, a group of squealing, laughing girls ran up to them. Introductions were made so quickly and with such enthusiasm that Aniela immediately began to relax.

"These are my friends," Judy said. "I told them all about you."

"Hi, Nellie!" one girl cried, touching her arm with fingernails painted bright red. Aniela thought her name was Bertha, but couldn't really remember. "What are the Nazis like? Are they as horrible as we hear?"

Aniela nodded. "They are monsters. They made my best friend Edith and her family run away, because they were Jewish. They took away my piano teacher, Stefan, and I will never see either of them again."

Suddenly, Aniela felt very sad. She bowed her head and bit her lip. So many nice things had happened to her in the last few days, but what of Stefan and Edith? Perhaps Stefan had been tortured at the very same time she was trying on that fancy angora sweater the other day!

The girls seemed to realize how distressed she was, for two of them put arms around her shoulders.

"Oh, let's not talk about the boring old Nazis," said one chubby girl. Aniela remembered her name was Lisa.

"Yes, there are much better things to talk about," said the girl to her right, a redhead named Becky. "Like . . . Tommy Dorsey!"

"And that cute guy that sings with him now," Judy said. "Frank . . . Frank . . . oh, what's his name?"

"Frank Sinatra!" two other girls cried in unison.

"Frank Sinatra?" Aniela asked.

"Come to my house this afternoon," Becky offered. "I'll spin one of his records for you."

"Spin his records?" Aniela repeated, not really understanding.

The girls giggled.

"Nellie, you're so funny," Judy said. "Don't worry, you'll be up on all the modern talk before you know it!"

Other kids passed them in the hall, and some glanced curiously at the newcomer. A few boys whispered and nudged each other.

"Just what we need," said one boy with a faceful of pale red freckles, "another Polack invading our school."

Aniela felt her heart beat faster. This boy had a hateful attitude, just like the Nazis back in Warsaw. Would he make trouble for her?

"For your information, Donny Greer," Judy said in a snooty tone, "we're called 'Poles,' not 'Polacks.' "

"You should be called 'losers,' " said Donny Greer.

Another boy stepped forward.

"Hey, Donny," he said. "What's the difference between a Polack and a pigeon?"

Aniela looked at her friends. "I don't understand that strange question."

Bertha gave Aniela's arm a tug and pulled her down the hall.

"Pay no attention to them," Bertha said.

"Donny Greer is a moron," said Judy.

"All the boys in seventh grade are dopes," Becky agreed. "I like older boys much better."

"Do you know my cousin Hank Kubek?" Aniela asked.

The girls nodded.

"He's in eighth grade," Becky said. "I think he's kinda cute."

Aniela thought of how mean Hank had been, but before she could say a word the bell rang. Mrs. Smith was as nice as her new friends had promised, and by the end of the class Aniela knew she would like American school very, very much.

When she got home, Aunt Elzie asked about her first day of seventh grade.

"I had a lot of fun, Aunt Elzie," Aniela said. "My new teacher is very pleasant, and I made new friends! I need to ask Papa if I can go to one girl's house to turn records."

Aunt Elzie laughed. "I think you mean 'spin records.' That's another slang expression the kids use."

"Oh, yes," Aniela said. "Judy said it means to play a record. Where is Papa, so I can ask him?"

"Your father has gone to apply for a job," Aunt Elzie said. She stood at the kitchen counter, chopping up vegetables. "Your Uncle Stan thought he could find him work at the slaughterhouse."

"Papa knows all about meat," Aniela said.

"Yes, I know, dear," Aunt Elzie said. "But I'm sure he'd say it was all right to go. You have a good time, and be home by six for dinner."

Aniela gave her aunt a kiss on the cheek. Aunt Elzie smelled of vanilla.

"Thank you," she said.

She went back out again, walking as fast as the icy sidewalk allowed. She couldn't wait to join Judy, Becky, and her other new friends!

Chapter Twelve

AS the weeks passed, Aniela enjoyed her life in America more and more. Every day after school, she met with her new friends. She loved to listen to all the new songs they played on their record players, especially the music of Glenn Miller. Judy said his music was called "Swing," and it was like nothing Aniela had ever heard. It was so lively and joyous. Aunt Elzie often played the music of Paderewski, or Henryk Wieniawski, or Frederic Chopin, but hearing those Polish musicians made Aniela sad and homesick. Whenever their songs came on the radio, she had to fight tears. Glenn Miller, Tommy Dorsey, Bing Crosby, and Frank Sinatra made her happy.

Still, all the happy music in the world could never erase the pain she felt each time she thought of Stefan,

Edith, and Jadzia. If only she could play piano again, perhaps that might ease her pain. But who could ever be as good a teacher as her beloved Stefan?

Aniela's favorite class at school was music. The children sang while their music teacher, Mrs. Harris, played an old upright piano. One day, she noticed Aniela gazing longingly at the piano. When class was finished, she asked her to stay for a moment.

"Aniela, there are tears in your eyes," she said with a kind smile. "Does 'America the Beautiful' move you that much?"

Aniela quickly wiped at her eyes.

"No, Mrs. Harris," she said. "It isn't the song. It's the piano. I used to play when I lived in Warsaw. But the Nazis took my piano teacher away."

Mrs. Harris frowned. "I'm sorry, Aniela. I've heard of the terrible things they've done there."

She turned to gather up her sheet music. When she looked at Aniela again, she was smiling.

"Why don't you take lessons here?" she suggested. "I know of a fine piano teacher."

"It wouldn't be the same," Aniela said. "Stefan was the best teacher ever."

"I know, dear," Mrs. Harris said, "but if you love piano, you should never give it up. Why don't you talk to your father and ask him what he thinks?"

Aniela promised that she would. As the day went on, she thought more and more of Mrs. Harris's words. *If you love piano, you should never give it up.* And hadn't Stefan himself once said that not playing her music was like giving in to the Nazis? If she refused to continue lessons here in America, wasn't it almost as if the Nazis had followed her here? She decided she did want to take lessons again. She was certain that was exactly what Stefan would want, too.

DINNER at the Kubek house was always a lively affair, with a lot of talking. Only Papa, tired after a long day, remained quiet. But he gave everyone else his full attention. He laughed when Leo told a funny story, and nodded with sympathy as Hank groaned about a particularly difficult geography test.

"And what of your day, Aniela?" he asked Aniela.

"We had music today, Papa," Aniela said. "That's my favorite class."

"I like science and math," Hank said. "Music is a waste of my time."

"Music is never a waste!" Aniela cried.

"Hank, be quiet and pass the cauliflower this way," said Uncle Stan.

"What songs are you learning now, Aniela?" Aunt Elzie asked.

" 'America the Beautiful' is one," Aniela said.

Aunt Elzie nodded. "Oh, yes. One of my favorites."

"And we're also learning a song called 'Home on the Range,' " Aniela said. "Mrs. Harris says it's an American folk song."

She looked at Uncle Stan. "Have you ever seen a buffalo?"

Hank laughed out loud. "There aren't any buffalos here!"

"Yes, but I have seen them," Uncle Stan said. "Years ago, I travelled through the Southwest."

"Maybe I'll be able to see all of America someday," Aniela said.

Papa reached for the water pitcher and refilled his glass. Then he said: "Aniela, do you also sing the folk songs of our own land?"

"Oh, yes, Papa," Aniela said. She thought this might be a good time to mention the piano lessons. "Papa, Mrs. Harris says she knows of a good piano teacher . . ."

Suddenly, Papa yawned and rubbed his eyes.

"Excuse me," he said. "It's been such a long day, and I am tired. Aniela, we can talk about this tomorrow."

He got up and left the room. Aniela saw that his limp was worse than ever. He walked with his head bowed forward, as if he was too exhausted to pick it up. When he was gone, Aunt Elzie spoke.

"Poor Max," she said. "He works so many long, hard hours. It's just wearing him out."

"There is no other work for him here, Elzie," Uncle Stan said. "It was hard enough to get that job for him, since he is not a citizen."

Aunt Elzie stood up. "Aniela, would you help me with the dishes?"

Aniela picked up an empty platter and followed her

into the kitchen. Aunt Elzie took two aprons from the hooks on the wall and handed one to Aniela.

"I needed to speak to you privately," she said. "Aniela, you see how very tired your father is, don't you?"

Aniela nodded. She gazed at Aunt Elzie, and wondered if there was bad news. Her aunt looked so serious.

"It isn't just the long hours at the slaughterhouse," she said. "Do you know that you don't have much money left?"

"Papa never said a thing, Aunt Elzie," Aniela told her. Papa never discussed finances with her.

"He spent most of his life savings getting you here to America," Aunt Elzie replied. "When he came to our house, there was only a few dollars left in his pocket. Aniela, he gave up so much to rescue you from the Nazis."

Tears began to form in Aniela's eyes. "He sold the butcher shop, Aunt Elzie. That was his store for even longer than I have been here, and he had to sell it! He was greatly admired in Warsaw, but now he has to work in a horrible slaughterhouse."

She bit her lip to keep the tears from falling. "It isn't fair! Papa worked so hard all his life, and for what? So those devils could take it all from him?"

"He did it for you, dear," Aunt Elzie said, "and nothing would make him happier than to see you happy. That is why I must talk to you. Aniela, he can't afford to pay for piano lessons. And if he knows you are unhappy about that, it will break his heart."

Now the tears really did fall. "Oh, Aunt Elzie! I don't want him to be unhappy! I'll forget about piano lessons, I really will. I won't say another word about them."

"That's a good girl," Aunt Elzie said. "Don't be discouraged. Who knows what the future might bring? Where there's life, there's hope."

She turned to the sink and filled the basin with soapy water. She washed, and Aniela dried. All the while, Aniela thought about Papa. What was his day like? When she was in school, happy with her friends, did he suffer over hot vats where they boiled the pigs? As she played in the schoolyard, did he haul heavy sides of beef? She felt terrible that she had even mentioned piano lessons. Poor Papa!

She dreamed of her old home that night. She was seated at the piano, with Stefan at her side. The music was a confusing blend. No sooner would she play one stanza of Chopin then her fingers would switch to Beethoven. It sounded awful, and in her dream, Aniela cried.

"Stefan, it sounds terrible! I need lessons!"

"No more lessons," Stefan said. "Never again, never again, never again . . ."

She woke with a start. The sun was shining, but it was Saturday and she didn't have to get up yet. Still, she couldn't lie in bed. When she did, her mind was just too full of sad thoughts. So she got up and went into the kitchen to make her breakfast. No one else was up yet.

When Aniela was finished with her cereal she washed her dish and put it in the drainer. Then she went outside to fill the birdfeeders that Uncle Stan had strung on a small tree. No sooner had she gone back in the house than dozens of birds flew down for their own breakfast. She saw sparrows and chickadees, and even counted six bluejays. Two cardinals appeared, and a flock of mourning doves. How lovely they were! Aniela wondered what it might be like to be a bird, to never have a worry.

"How come you're up so early?" she heard Hank say.

She frowned at him. "Don't be mean to me. I don't want to listen to that today."

Hank poured himself a bowl of cornflakes, then sat down. He made a lot of noise when he ate, but Aniela didn't say anything.

"You want to ride my bike today?" Hank asked.

The question was so unexpected that at first Aniela didn't believe she'd heard it.

"Huh?"

"I asked if you wanted to ride my bike," Hank said. "It's a boy's bike, but I think you can ride it if I adjust the seat."

"I'd like that," Aniela said. "I used to have a bicycle in Warsaw."

A short time later, Hank stood in front of the house and watched her ride up and down the street. Even with the seat pushed all the way down, she could hardly reach the pedals. But it was so much fun, and she was laughing when she finally rolled the bike back up to the Kubek's garage.

"Thank you, Hank," she said.

Hank just shrugged his shoulders.

"Hank?" Aniela asked as they walked to the back door, "why are you being nice to me now?"

"Can't a guy be nice to his own cousin?"

Aniela shrugged. "Of course, but . . ."

"Mom told me that you couldn't take piano lessons," Hank interrupted. "And that's real important to you, isn't it?"

"I want it more than anything."

"Yeah, that's how I feel about basketball," Hank said. "But we didn't have the money for me to join the team this year. That's 'cause my folks needed it to help you and Uncle Max."

"Oh!" Aniela cried. "You lost something you love because of us?"

She felt bad to hear that. Now she understood why Hank had been so mean to her.

"It's okay," Hank said. "Forget it. I guess we all have to give up some stuff these days. Pop says the Depression should be over soon, now that factories are opening to make stuff for the war in Europe. I bet I get on the team next September!"

"I hope you do," Aniela said.

If Hank was able to join basketball, that meant she might be able to take her piano lessons, too. All they could do was hope.

WINTER seemed to last a long time that year, so when the first crocuses finally pushed through the hard ground, Aniela thought they were a beautiful sight. They were soon followed by hyacinths and tulips and daffodils. The grass sprung up and light green baby leaves appeared on the trees. One morning in late March, Aunt Elzie told Aniela to leave her jacket at home. The sky was bright and blue, and sunlight glistened on Aniela's dark curls. When she met Judy to walk to school, her friend was wearing a pale green dress with puffed sleeves.

"That's so pretty," Aniela said admiringly. "I wish I had a dress like that."

"Easter's coming up soon," Judy said. "Maybe your aunt will buy you a new Sunday dress for the holiday."

They met Bertha, Becky, and Lisa at school. Becky had a new movie magazine, and she showed off a poster of Frank Sinatra that had been stapled into the middle.

"Is there anything about Clark Gable in there?" Aniela asked.

"Oh, there's something about him," Becky said. She sighed. "But I like Frankie better. He's the dreamiest, isn't he?"

Aniela shrugged. She still thought Clark Gable was handsome. Aunt Elzie had taken her to see *Gone with the Wind* last month, and she'd had daydreams about the handsome actor carrying her in his arms. Only it hadn't been Atlanta they were fleeing. It was

Warsaw, and Gable bravely protected her from the Nazis. But she didn't tell anybody about this. She worried they would think she was silly.

It was Tuesday, her favorite day of the week because that was the day her class had music lessons. The five girls always stood together. Becky mumbled her songs because she could hardly sing at all, and Bertha struggled with the high notes. Aniela and Lisa had alto voices, and they could harmonize well enough. But Judy was the one with the beautiful soprano voice, and Aniela loved to hear her.

"Someday," she whispered to Judy as Mrs. Harris prepared the next musicpiece, "I'll play and you'll sing with me onstage."

"At Symphony Center over in Chicago," Judy agreed.

"And then Carnegie Hall in New York City," Aniela said.

Mrs. Harris was a small woman who almost disappeared behind the school's upright piano. She raised herself taller and focused directly on Aniela and Judy. Aniela lowered her eyes, and Judy shifted uncomfortably.

"No talking, please," said Mrs. Harris. "Open your books to page seven."

She began to play, and the children sang. It was an old Polish folk song, one Aniela could play with her eyes closed. Mrs. Harris played nicely, but Aniela was able to pick out mistakes in her work that no one else would have noticed. She would never tell her teacher that, though. That would be disrespectful.

"Aniela Kaminski," Mrs. Harris said suddenly.

Aniela's heart skipped a beat. Had Mrs. Harris seen the way she cringed at that last sour note?

"Yes, ma'am?"

"Come over here, dear," said Mrs. Harris.

She spoke so kindly that Aniela knew at once she was not in trouble. But what did the teacher want? Aniela looked at Judy, who only shrugged. Then she moved through the group of children and went to stand by the piano.

"Do you know how to play this song?" she asked.

"Oh, yes!" Aniela said. "It's one of my favorites."

"Then you can play for us," said Mrs. Harris. "Here, sit down next to me."

Aniela slid onto the bench. Mrs. Harris counted—one, two, three—and Aniela began to play. The notes were rich and strong and pure. The children were so surprised that they didn't even sing along. Aniela stopped in the middle of the song.

"What's wrong?" she asked.

"Aniela," Mrs. Harris said, "I had no idea you played like that."

She looked at the class. "I think we have a virtuoso in our school!"

Judy began to clap, and then Bertha and Becky and Lisa. Soon the whole class applauded. Aniela stared at the piano keys and smiled, blushing with pride.

"Play something else, Nellie," a boy named Mark asked.

"Yeah, play a new song!" said Donna Kennedy.

Mrs. Harris gave her a nod of approval, and Aniela played. The children soon began to sing again. Most everyone was disappointed when the bell rang, especially Aniela. Only Donny Greer, who had been making faces at her the whole time she played, was glad to run out.

"Dumb showoff Polack," he said to her as he went by.

"I heard that, Donald Greer," Mrs. Harris said. "You will stay after school for an hour today."

"But Mrs. Harris!" Donny whined. "My mother will kill me!"

"I doubt that, young man," Mrs. Harris said, "but I'm sure you'll be in a lot of trouble when she hears of the nasty word you used."

Aniela just stood there with her mouth open. Why was Donny so hateful to her?

"Don't pay any attention to him," Judy said, tugging at her arm. "He's a dope. He's mean and he hates everyone."

Aniela felt hurt by his words, but she was soon smiling as her friends showered her with praise.

"Nellie, you never told us you played like that," Lisa exclaimed. "You sound better than some of those guys who play on the radio!"

"I'm glad I can still play at all," Aniela said. "I

thought I sounded awful today. It's been so long since I had lessons, or a piano to practice on."

"I thought you were terrific," Bertha praised. "I think you should take lessons again."

"I want to, but Papa can't afford a teacher and my aunt and uncle don't even have a piano," Aniela explained.

She suddenly felt very sad, and very homesick. It had been fun to play for her class, but now all it did was remind her of how much she missed Warsaw, and her old life, when Stefan gave her lessons three days a week in exchange for his room and board.

Chapter Thirteen

PREPARATIONS for Easter in the Kubek home began three days early, on Holy Thursday. School was out, so Aniela helped Aunt Elzie bake a Polish treat, *babka*, a rich yeast bread dotted with raisins. She grated orange and lemon peels to flavor it, while Aunt Elzie kneaded the dough.

"Your grandmother gave me this recipe," Aunt Elzie said. "It's a secret family recipe that she got from her own grandmother."

"That's funny," Aniela said, "because *babka* means *grandmother* in Polish!"

"Mama always said a housewife is judged by how well her *babka* rises," Aunt Elzie said. She laughed and added, "I remember when your own mama and I would compete with each other, to see who had the highest, lightest bread!"

"Who won, Aunt Elzie?"

"Sometimes me, sometimes Helena," Aunt Elzie said. She gazed out the kitchen window with a dreamy look, as if she was thinking of those old days. "But neither one of us ever made as fine a *babka* as our mother, your grandmother."

It took forty minutes to knead the dough to perfection. Aniela took turns with her aunt, until at last Aunt Elzie declared it was ready to be left to rise. No sooner had they cleaned the counter than she brought out poppy seeds, nuts, and more ingredients to make poppy seed and nut bread. By the time they were through baking for the day, Aniela felt as if her arms might drop right off.

On Good Friday, Aniela's and Judy's families walked to St. Stanislaus Cathedral for services. All the holy statues were covered in purple cloth, and everything was solemn in memory of Christ's Passion. As she breathed in the smell of incense and prayed with the congregation, Aniela thought of her friends back in Poland. She knew she was lucky to be able to worship as she chose here in America. Back in Poland, any ceremony Jadzia might be having would have to be done in secret because of the Nazis. And even though she was at a Catholic service, she also wondered if Edith had been able to celebrate her Jewish Passover, wherever she was.

As they walked home together, Aniela asked Judy, "Can you come to my aunt's house?"

"Not today," Judy said. "I have to help Mom make the preparations for Easter. But come to my house tomorrow. I want to show you the dress I'm wearing on Easter Sunday, and my new hat, too!"

Aniela said that she would. She wished she could have a new dress, too. But Aunt Elzie had already bought her school clothes. It would be wrong to expect more.

Aunt Elzie made lunch for everyone. Papa ate quickly. He'd been excused from the slaughterhouse to attend services—his boss was also Catholic and went to his own church for services—but he had to get back to finish the day. He gave Aniela a kiss when he finished, and left.

"Poor Papa," Aniela said. "Not a full day off, even on Good Friday."

"There is simply too much work to be done," Uncle Stan said.

Aniela had learned that Uncle Stan worked as an accountant in a small bank. He didn't have to go back to a dirty, steaming-hot factory today. She thought of Papa's clean, cool butcher shop and, for just a moment, wished they were back in Poland again. But only for a moment, because the Poland they had loved was no longer there.

"Mommy, can I go to Billy's house?" Leo asked.

"All right," Aunt Elzie said. "But you be back by five. What are your plans, Hank?"

"I thought I'd see if any of the guys want to play ball at the park," Hank said. "You want to come watch, Nellie?"

Aunt Elzie put a hand on her arm before she could answer. "I was hoping you would help me make the *paska* today, Aniela."

"I'd like that," Aniela said, smiling at her. "Sorry, Hank. I'll watch you another time, okay?"

"Okay," said Hank.

Aniela was happy they were friends now. Hank and Leo were like the brothers she never had.

After the lunch dishes were cleared away, Uncle Stan went outside to tinker with the engine of the family car, which had been making strange noises lately. Aniela and Aunt Elzie took everything out to prepare the *paska*.

"It's so nice to have a girl to help me," Aunt Elzie said. "Men are not permitted to help with the *paska,* you know."

"We never made it at home," Aniela said. "Mr. Kozmyk, the baker, would bring it to our house. I don't know if the ladies who worked for him baked the bread. But why can't men do it, Aunt Elzie?"

"Because if they do," Aunt Elzie said with a very serious expression, "their mustaches turn gray, and the dough doesn't rise!"

She began to laugh, and Aniela laughed with her.

"It's just an old superstition," Aunt Elzie said. "But your grandmother truly believed in it." She sighed. "So many traditions are lost when you emigrate to a new country."

She began to fashion a cross from dough.

"But many of our ways are still with us," she said.

"Adolf Hitler would take them all away," Aniela said.

Aunt Elzie held a slender finger to her lips. "Shh! No talk of such a devil on this holy day, dear."

She lay the cross over the top of the unbaked bread. "Here, let me show you how to make a little dough flower."

Soon, the dough cross was surrounded by flowers and birds. Aniela helped her aunt to lift the pan carefully and place it in the oven to bake. When it came out, it was a beautiful golden brown.

"It's a work of art, Elzie," Uncle Stan said when he came inside to take a peek.

"It's wonderful," Aniela agreed.

"If you want to see something wonderful," Aunt Elzie said, "wait until we color eggs tonight!"

Back in Poland, eggs had been such a rare treat that Aniela was always amazed that they were readily available in America. That night, Aunt Elzie set out several dozen. Everyone gathered around the table, even Papa, to color them. Leo made *malowanki*, eggs of one color. Aniela and Hank decorated their eggs with shining bits of fabric and colored paper. Aunt Elzie and Uncle Stan used little pointed instruments to etch designs into their colored eggs. But it was Papa who was the real artist. He drew fancy designs on his eggs with wax, and then carefully colored each section with a different dye. When the wax was melted away, everyone marveled at the remarkable egg called a *pisanki*. Set against a black background, the multicolored designs were strikingly beautiful.

"Oh, Papa," Aniela said, "how could I have forgotten what a master you are!"

"All the eggs are very beautiful, little one," Papa said. "And how lovely they will be on our table on Sunday morning!"

"And even more beautiful when they are blessed by the priest tomorrow," Uncle Stan said.

Holy Saturday brought another church service. This time, the people brought baskets full of *paska*, horseradish, sausages, and other foods. The priest sprinkled the baskets with holy water to consecrate them. Aniela had to smile at the way little Leo held his own basket, his freckled face so solemn. Aunt Elzie had bought a little sugar lamb for him, and he held it in a basket full of eggs as if it were a real pet.

Later that day, Aunt Elzie called Aniela into her bedroom. There were two large boxes on the bed.

"Open them, dear," she said.

Brimming with curiosity, Aniela took the lid off the largest box. Inside was a dress of the most beautiful rose color she'd ever seen. It had a lace collar and puffed sleeves of a light, sheer fabric. She stared at it for a moment, not really understanding what she was supposed to do.

"Take it out, Aniela," Aunt Elzie said. "It's for you."

"For me?" Aniela gasped. "It's for me? Oh, Aunt Elzie! It's beautiful!"

She gave her aunt a big hug. "But . . . but you've been too generous with me."

"Nonsense," said Aunt Elzie. "It's your very first Easter in America, and I want you to be properly dressed for Easter Sunday mass. Go ahead, dear. Take it out and try it on."

Aunt Elzie helped her unbutton the back of her sweater. Aniela slipped the pretty dress over her head and stood in front of a large mirror as her aunt zipped her up and tied the sash into a frothy bow. She turned this way and that, smiling as she admired her reflection.

"It's so beautiful," she said. "I can't believe it! I'll be as pretty as Judy tomorrow."

"Prettier," Aunt Elzie insisted. "Now . . ."

She opened the smaller box and took out a straw Easter bonnet. It was decorated with tiny pink and white roses. Aniela put it on, and her smile grew even bigger.

"I never had a hat like this before," she admitted.

"Then it's about time you did," Aunt Elzie declared.

How proud Aniela felt as they walked to church the next day. Judy squealed with admiration to see her new outfit. They met up with Bertha, Becky, and Lisa. It was a perfect April morning, the sky blue and the grass dotted with tulips, daffodils, and hyacinths. Everyone was full of joy, and church bells rang out to celebrate the Resurrection of Jesus Christ. During Mass, Aniela said prayers for her friends back in Poland.

Let them be hearing bells like these, she thought. Let the Nazis go away and may Stefan and Edith be free again!

Back home, everyone helped set up the table. Aniela was certain she'd never seen such a magnificent spread in her whole life. They set out the cakes and breads Aniela had helped to bake. Baskets of colored eggs were surrounded by plates of sausages and ham. Leo took his small sugar lamb from its basket and put it beside a larger one in the center of the table. Uncle Stan himself had made a *cwikla*—a dish of beets and horseradish.

"Let's sit down and share eggs," he said. "There's no better way to extend our good wishes to each other."

"Pick my egg, Daddy!" Leo cried. "Pick my egg."

Laughing, Uncle Stan took an egg from Leo's basket. He cracked it open, then sprinkled it with salt and pepper.

"You take the first bite, Aniela," he said.

Aniela smiled, took a bite, then passed the egg to Hank. Everyone at the table took a bite, and somehow one egg was shared among six people. Next, Aunt Elzie lifted the platter that held the *paska*, the fancy, decorated bread she and Aniela had made on Good Friday. Each person broke off a piece, sharing the bread the priest had blessed at Holy Saturday services.

Everyone enjoyed the wonderful meal. Aniela had three helpings of ham, making Hank laugh at her.

"Never saw a girl eat like that," he said.

"We don't get much meat back home now," Aniela told him.

Hank's smile faded. "Sorry. I forgot about that."

"Let's say a prayer for our fellow countrymen," Papa suggested. "That they may know bounty and joy as we do now."

Everyone bowed heads and Papa said a prayer.

"Next year," he said, when he finished, "we will go back to Poland and have a celebration there. Warsaw is beautiful in the springtime."

Aniela felt tears rise in her. Warsaw wasn't beautiful at all now. It was a nightmare of bombed-out buildings and Nazi tanks and trucks. But she bit her lip and fought the tears. She wouldn't cry today, not on this most joyous of all occasions. She would not let Nazi cruelty touch her here in America.

It was an Easter she knew she would never forget. After the meal, she went to Judy's house to listen to records. She wore her new bonnet and dress and wished she'd never have to take them off. It was so wonderful to be here in this safe, happy place, so far away from the dark, hateful world of Nazi oppression!

Chapter Fourteen

THERE was a week's vacation after Easter Sunday. Uncle Stan took Tuesday off and drove everyone into downtown Chicago to go sightseeing. Only Papa remained behind, working as hard as ever.

Chicago was full of wonderful old buildings. Aniela was fascinated by the Reid Murdoch building, a place where food was processed and stored.

"Look how big that clock is!" she cried, pointing at the tower that stood on top of the building.

"The building is seven floors," Uncle Stan said, "and the clock tower stands another three stories tall."

"Gee, I sure wish I could work on one of those barges," Leo said. The building was on the waterfront, and boats waited at the loading docks that were built into its lower floors.

"Maybe you will one day, Leo," Aunt Elzie said.

"I don't want to work on a boat," Hank said. "I want to be a scientist. Maybe even work in one of the museums here."

Aunt Elzie put an arm around Aniela's shoulders.

"How about you, dear?" she asked. "What do you want to be when you grow up?"

"A pianist like my mama," Aniela said without a moment's hesitation.

Right away, she was sorry she'd said such a thing. What was the use of it, when she might not ever have lessons? She shrugged.

"Well, maybe . . . someday," she said.

Aunt Elzie hugged her. "I wouldn't be surprised."

Later that day, they visited Soldier Field, a huge arena on the Chicago lakefront. It was dedicated to soldiers who had fought in World War I. Aniela thought of the soldiers who had died fighting for Polish freedom. Would anyone ever build such a remarkable monument to them?

At dinnertime, Aniela tasted her first slice of pizza, in a little restaurant. She really liked it, and Uncle Stan promised they'd have some again one day. By the time they returned home, Aniela was so tired she went straight to bed. It had been a wonderful day, but she knew she would have enjoyed it more if Papa had been there, too.

ON Wednesday morning, Judy called and asked if Aniela could go to the movies.

"*The Wizard of Oz* is playing," she said.

Aniela laughed. "But you told me you saw it twice already!"

"And I really want to see it again," Judy insisted. "It's my favorite!"

"That's because you have the same name as Judy Garland," Aniela said.

"Please come see it with me," Judy urged.

"Oh, I don't know," Aniela said, although she wished she could say yes. "I don't have any money."

She would never ask Papa for money for something as trivial as a movie. Not when Papa all but dragged himself home each night, too exhausted to do much but eat and go to bed. And Aunt Elzie had already been too generous with her this Easter. Aniela thought of her new dress and hat, carefully hung in her closet. No, it would be greedy to ask for more.

"I'll treat you," Judy said. "I just got my allowance. Please, Nellie, say you'll go? Bertha and Becky and Lisa will be there, too!"

So Aniela asked for permission, and Aunt Elzie gladly gave it.

"But if Judy is going to treat you to a ticket," she said, "it's only right that you should treat her to popcorn!"

She opened her purse and produced two shining quarters. Leo, who played nearby with a windup Popeye car, gasped.

"Can I have a quarter, too?" he asked.

"My garden is full of weeds, Leo," his mother said. "I'll pay you a quarter for pulling them."

Leo moaned. Aunt Elzie winked at Aniela as if to say she knew her garden would be weeded before the morning was through.

It was such a warm day that Aniela did not even need a sweater. She met up with Judy, and together they went on to Becky's house. Soon all the girls were together, laughing and talking. As they turned the corner onto Caron Street, where the United Theater stood, they discovered a long line leading up to the ticket window.

"Oh, ugh," Lisa groaned. "There's Donny Greer."

"I don't like that boy at all," Judy said. "I hope he sits far away from us."

Aniela thought about the mean thing he'd whispered to her that day she played piano for her music class. When they got inside the theater, she was glad when he went up into the balcony. She thought he was a little scary, although she never said this to her friends. They'd think she was silly.

Aniela watched with fascination as a newsreel brought them up to date on the war in Europe. She was scared to hear that the Germans had marched into Norway and Denmark. But she pushed those worries aside when the cartoon started. She was here to have fun with her friends, not to let the Nazis make her sad. She laughed with the other children at a *Tom and Jerry* cartoon. When Judy Garland sang "Over the Rainbow" in the movie, Aniela had to wipe tears from her eyes. And she thought there was never more amazing a sight than when Dorothy Gale walked through the doorway of her farmhouse, passing from a dreary, sepia-tone world into a land of magnificent color.

When it was over, everyone chattered about the movie as they left the theater.

"I hope I don't have nightmares about that witch!" Becky said with a shudder.

"The newsreel was scarier than the movie," Bertha said. "Those Nazis seem to be very powerful!"

"They're spreading over Europe like a disease," Judy said, making a disgusted face.

"I wish a house would drop on Adolf Hitler!" Lisa said, and the girls laughed.

"Well, they aren't as powerful as we are here in America," Bertha insisted. "They'd never dare try to start a war with us."

"I hope you're right, Bertha," Aniela said. "I don't know what I'd do if they came over here to fight."

"Oh, let's stop talking about the war," Judy insisted. "Come on, Nellie. My mother baked a strawberry pie this morning. Maybe she'll let us have a piece."

They passed a dress shop as they walked home, and stopped for a moment to admire the display. Mannequins dressed in the latest spring fashions posed elegantly. Aniela thought of Mrs. Ryzop, who had owned the dress shop on her street in Warsaw, and who had been shot by the Nazis. She turned away from the window. She did not want to think about such sad things. As she did so, she saw Donny Greer and two of his friends come around the corner.

"Oh, no," she said.

Judy turned around and saw the boys, too.

"Let's go," she urged.

Bertha let out a moan, and the girls all walked away as quickly as they could.

"Hey, Polack!"

"Flake off, Donny," Lisa snapped.

"Why don't you go back to Poland where you belong, Kaminski?" Donny yelled.

"It's a free country, Donny Greer," Judy said. "Nellie has as much right to be here as you."

"She got me into big trouble with Mrs. Harris!" Donny said. "And with my mom, too! She's a big show-off. And my daddy says guys like her father are big, dumb losers who come here and take jobs away from real Americans!"

Aniela was shocked. What job had her father taken away? Hours in a steaming hot, bad-smelling slaughterhouse? Who would really want a job like that unless they were forced to take it, because there was nothing else?

"That isn't fair!" she cried. "My papa works very, very hard! And he is not a big, dumb loser!"

"I say he is," Donny sneered. He looked at his friends. "Right, guys?"

Donny's two friends, boys Aniela did not know, nodded.

"Take that back, Donny Greer," Lisa said, stepping forward with her fists clenched.

"Make me!" Donny laughed.

Lisa stepped forward to swing at him. But Donny was faster, and he gave her a good, hard push. Lisa fell to the ground. Before she could get up, Donny tried to kick her. Aniela moved between them and took the blow of his foot in her shin.

"Greer, cut it out!" cried one of the other boys. "You ain't supposed to hit a girl!"

Lisa got up quickly. By now, Becky was crying. Bertha was already half a block away, waiting for her friends to come, too. Judy grabbed the fist Aniela had balled up to hit Donny.

"Let's just go, Nellie," she insisted. "Dopes like him aren't worth it!"

"I'm not done!" Donny yelled.

"Who cares?" Judy said. "Just go away and leave us alone!"

Donny stepped forward again. Becky cried even louder. But the other two boys grabbed Donny and held him back. The girls were able to get away. By the time they reached Judy's, Aniela was very upset.

"Why did those boys have to be so mean?" she asked her friends as they sat around Judy's kitchen table eating strawberry pie. Judy's mother had poured big glasses of Ovaltine for them, too.

"Because they're stupid, that's why," Judy said.

"I thought there wasn't any hate in America," Aniela said. "I thought there wasn't any prejudice."

Bertha sighed. "There are bad people, everywhere, Nellie."

It made Aniela very sad to know this was true. It didn't matter where you went, there would always be someone who didn't like you, just because of the country you came from, or your religion (Aniela thought of poor Edith), or the color of your skin. Maybe America wasn't such a great place, after all.

"WHY are you looking so glum, little one?" Papa asked her as she did her homework that night.

"I saw someone being mean to a kid today," Aniela said. "He used a bad word against the Polish people."

Papa nodded sadly. "I know the word. *Polack*. I hear it enough at work."

"What should I . . ." Aniela stopped herself. She didn't want Papa to know she was the one called that bad name. He would worry about her, and he had so much else to think about these days. "What should someone do if they hear that word?"

"Hold your head up high," Papa said, "and remember the fine history of our people. Think of the great Polish people through history—Copernicus, Chopin, Marie Curie, and so many others. Then you'll know that people only talk like that because they don't know any better."

The phone rang just then, and Aunt Elzie answered it. When she hung up, she came into the living room and said it had been Mrs. Harris, the music teacher.

"She called to ask if you would be home this evening," Aunt Elzie said. "Now, why do you suppose your music teacher wants to talk to you in the middle of Easter vacation?"

"I don't know, Aunt Elzie," Aniela said. She was surprised, too. Was it possible Mrs. Harris had heard what Donny did to her this afternoon?

She was so full of curiosity that she hardly tasted her dinner that night. Shortly after seven, there was a knock at the door. Hank opened it. Mrs. Harris was standing there, dressed in a pretty pink coat and matching hat. Aniela saw a big white delivery truck behind her.

"Hank, would you get your father and your uncle?" Mrs. Harris asked. "I have something heavy that needs to be brought into the house."

"Oh, my Papa shouldn't lift anything heavy," Aniela said. "He has a bad leg."

Papa, who had come up behind Aniela, patted her on the shoulder.

"I would lift a building for you, little one," he said. "This surprise for you is not nearly as heavy!"

"For me?" Aniela asked. "A surprise for me?"

Now Aunt Elzie told her she knew exactly what Mrs. Harris had for her.

"I kept it secret because Mrs. Harris wanted to surprise you," Aunt Elzie said.

Aniela watched as her father, uncle, and cousin took something out of the back of the truck. It was covered with a quilted blanket, but it didn't take long for her to realize what it was.

"Oh, my goodness!" she cried. "It's a piano!"

"Yes, Aniela," Mrs. Harris said.

"Wow, a real piano," Leo said. He held the door open.

Aniela stared at her teacher, hardly able to speak. "How . . ."

"Aniela," Mrs. Harris said, "you have a great talent. I could hardly believe my ears when you played for the class the other day. You are a prodigy."

"A what?"

"A child with a great gift," Aunt Elzie explained.

"And a gift like that should not be wasted," Mrs. Harris said.

The piano was rolled carefully into the house. Aunt Elzie pointed to a corner of the living room. Quickly, Aniela and Leo moved aside a chair.

"You will have to let it sit for a few days," Mrs. Harris said, "so that it can 'settle' itself. Then I'll send a tuner over."

"Mrs. Harris, I don't know what to say!" Aniela had tears in her eyes.

A simple "thank-you" didn't seem like enough for such a generous gift.

"It's a little worn out," Mrs. Harris said. "There was a fire at a church near my house, and the wood is singed. The parishioners bought a new piano, and this was just sitting in a back room. I'm friends with the minister, and he agreed to give it to me when I told him about you. And I've also made arrangements for lessons."

"Lessons!" Aniela said. But her smile quickly faded. How could Mrs. Harris offer lessons when she knew Papa could not pay for them?

"John Storton, one of the best teachers in town, is a widower with a young daughter," Mrs. Harris explained. "He sometimes needs a baby-sitter for her. He's willing to teach you in exchange for helping him with the three-year-old."

"Oh, I'd like that!" Aniela said. She couldn't believe her good fortune!

Epilogue

One Year Later

SO many things happened to Aniela and her father that next year. They passed their tests to become American citizens. Aniela took piano lessons every week in exchange for baby-sitting. Her new teacher was stricter and older than Stefan had been, but he was also kind and full of praise. He knew she would go far someday. Aniela often played at rallies and meetings that helped support the Polish cause. People even paid to hear her in concert, and her music helped raise almost a thousand dollars to send to the people of Poland!

There was bad news from her home. She learned that the Nazis had built a separate community for the Jews in Warsaw: a filthy, overcrowded place that was called The Ghetto. They forced all the Jews to go there, and anyone caught trying to sneak over the wall to freedom was shot. There was also talk of concentration camps, places where the Jewish people would be kept under control. At thirteen, Aniela could not even imagine what the Nazis meant by "under control." She only knew it would be horrible, and thanked God that Edith had escaped such a terrible fate. But hardly a day went by when she did not wonder what really happened to her friend, and to Stefan.

And then one day, a miracle happened. She was out in the garden helping Aunt Elzie trim her rose bushes. They both wore straw hats to keep the sun out of their eyes. Aunt Elzie pushed hers back a little with one gloved hand. She pointed her clippers at the walkway.

"Someone is coming," she said.

Aniela looked up. To her surprise, who should be walking toward them but Mr. Kozmyk, the baker, who had been her neighbor back in Warsaw! She dropped her own clippers and ran to greet him, pulling off her gloves along the way. She stuffed them into her apron pocket and threw her arms around the old man.

"Mr. Kozmyk! Mr. Kozmyk!" she cried. "You've come to America!"

"Hello, Aniela," said Mr. Kozmyk

Aniela stepped back. The baker looked much older than she remembered, and very tired. He put an arm around her shoulders and walked with her to meet Aunt Elzie. He felt heavy against her, and Aniela knew he was weak.

"Was it a difficult voyage, Mr. Kozmyk?" she asked.

"Long and hard," he said. "It is almost impossible to leave our country now. But that is a story for later."

Aunt Elzie came up to them. She had taken off her own gloves and her hat. Her clippers jutted from a pocket in her apron.

"This is a friend of Papa's from Warsaw," Aniela introduced. "He was our baker. His name is Mr. Kozmyk. Mr. Kozmyk, this is my aunt, Elzie Kubek."

The adults shook hands.

"Come inside for some iced tea," Aunt Elzie offered. "When did you arrive in America?"

"A few weeks ago," Mr. Kozmyk said. "I was staying in New Jersey with friends. But I have things to tell Max—and you, too, Aniela. So I took a plane ride here."

He shuddered. "I don't like airplanes at all. I never want to travel in one again!"

They entered the kitchen, and Aniela sat at the table with her neighbor. Aunt Elzie poured three glasses of iced tea and sat herself.

"What kind of things do you have to tell us, Mr. Kozmyk?" Aniela asked.

But Mr. Kozmyk would not say a word until Papa came home. Aunt Elzie and Uncle Stan invited him to stay for dinner. He told them how he'd seen the horrible things happening to the Jews, and how he knew he had to leave Warsaw before the Nazis found some reason to arrest him, too.

"Today the Jews, tomorrow—who knows?" he said. "These Nazis, they hate everyone. I have heard bad things about The Ghetto. People get sick and die in there because there isn't enough medicine. Babies go hungry. Sometimes, people on the outside climb the wall and give them food. But there is only so much we can do."

"What made you decide to leave Warsaw just at this time?" Papa asked.

Mr. Kozmyk put a bite of roast beef into his mouth. He savored it as if he'd never had any in his life, and might never have any again.

"It isn't just the Nazis," Mr. Kozmyk said. "There are traitors among our own people who do their bidding willingly enough. I brought some rolls to the ghetto wall, and was told not to give the food to the poor. Not by a Nazi, but by one of my own Polish customers! I was told to mind my own business. And I said, 'My starving friends and neighbors are my business.' "

"Good for you!" Uncle Stan said.

"What happened then?" Aniela asked.

"The next day, I went into my kitchen to find that all my flour and sugar had been knocked onto the floor and trampled. It wasn't Nazi boots this time—I know the pattern of those soles—but shoes that might have belonged to one of our own. I knew then that I had to escape. I took what little I had and made my way across the border into Germany."

"Germany!" Hank cried. "That was very dangerous, wasn't it?"

Mr. Kozmyk smiled at him. "I have blue eyes, you see. And my German is perfect. I easily passed for one of their own. But each day I moved across that country, I knew it could be my last. I finally made it into the

Netherlands and from there found my way to a ship bound for America. If not for the kind help of strangers, who helped me along the way, I would not be here."

Aniela finished her glass of milk. "Mr. Kozmyk, you said earlier you had something to tell Papa and me?"

"Yes, Aniela," Mr. Kozmyk said. "I have heard news of Stefan Olczak."

Aniela gasped. "Tell us, Mr. Kozmyk! Please—is he all right?"

"He is alive," Mr. Kozmyk said, "and doing as well as might be expected of a man in prison. He sends his love to you, Aniela, and asks that you keep him in your prayers."

"I pray for him every night," Aniela replied. She felt a mix of joy and sadness: joy that Stefan was alive, but sadness that he was not free.

"If that man is in prison, how did he get word out?" Hank wanted to know.

His father gave him a smile and a nod for asking such a good question.

"Stefan has many friends on the outside," Mr. Kozmyk said. "It was the way he was able to get Edith Lukowicz and her family out of the country, to safety. And the way he arranged for your own flight, Max."

Papa sighed and poked at his mashed potatoes with a fork. "He gave up his freedom and we have ours."

Aunt Elzie reached over and patted her brother-in-law's hand. "Chin up, Max. I'm sure the Nazis will soon be driven out and our people will be free again."

"I wish what you said would come true," Mr. Kozmyk said. "But if you were there, if you saw their power, you would believe they will be our conquerors forever."

"I bet if we Americans were fighting them . . ." Hank started to say.

"That isn't going to happen," Aunt Elzie said. "We'll never fight that war!"

Aniela didn't want to hear any more about the Nazis. She wanted to know about her friends.

"Mr. Kozmyk, do you know anything about the Kolbe family? About Jadzia?"

Mr. Kozmyk smiled sadly. "She misses you, Aniela. She asks about you all the time, but no one says anything. She came into the bakery one day to buy rolls for the guests at the inn, and she asked me if I knew what happened to you. There was a Nazi standing there, and I knew he was listening. But I gave her hand a squeeze, and she smiled. She realizes you had left the way Edith left, to a safer place. Perhaps, one day, you'll see each other again."

Aniela closed her eyes. In her mind, she saw herself and Edith and Jadzia walking with Stefan. Warsaw was beautiful and whole—there were no burned-out buildings and no red-and-black Nazi flags. Her friends were laughing, and Stefan's smile made him more handsome than ever.

"I don't know if I will see them again," she said, "but I will never forget them! Every time I play at a rally or a meeting, I'll think of them, and all our people!"

And if she never forgot them, Aniela thought, then perhaps one day they really would be free!

Author's Note

WORLD War II began in September 1939, when the German Army invaded Poland without any advanced warning or declaration of war. Although they fought as hard as they could, the Polish Army was no match for their enemy. Germany quickly took over the country. Adolf Hitler wanted to erase the Polish people from the face of the earth. He took away their rights, even the right to speak their own language. A year after the fall of Warsaw, all the Jewish people of that city were forced to move into overcrowded ghettos, where disease and hunger quickly took their toll. But that was nothing compared to the horrors that were to come. Under Nazi rule, over ten million people were murdered because they did not conform to Hitler's idea of a master race of perfect humans. Six million of these were of the Jewish faith. When we speak of the Holocaust, we remember these innocent people and how they suffered.

At the time this story takes place, many Americans did not want to become involved in the war in Europe. They remembered the terrible destruction of World War I and hoped to remain isolated from the troubles overseas. Then, on December 7, 1941, the Japanese bombed Pearl Harbor and declared war on the United States. America quickly took action and fought on both European and Asian fronts until 1945, when both Germany and Japan surrendered.